What had Tess expected, he wondered. A baby?

Since she was coming into town ten years after the child's birth, of course their daughter was going to be all grown up. Why did Tess look so astounded?

When Tess lifted her gaze to his, it was filled with silent, thunderous questions Dylan found quite bewildering. Her attention clamped once again on the daughter, she uttered a soft, breathy "Oh, my," turned and raced out the door.

"Wow," Erin said to him. "Who was that, Dad?"

Dylan didn't answer right away. Not because he meant to ignore his daughter's query, but because he didn't know what to say.

"That," he said at last with a slow, measured reluctance, "was your mother...."

Dear Reader,

In May 2000 Silhouette Romance will commemorate its twentieth anniversary! This line has always celebrated the essence of true love in a manner that blends classic themes and the challenges of romance in today's world into a reassuring, fulfilling novel. From the enchantment of first love to the wonder of second chance, a Silhouette Romance novel demonstrates the power of genuine emotion and the breathless connection that develops between a man and a woman as they discover each other. And this month's stellar selections are quintessential Silhouette Romance stories!

If you've been following LOVING THE BOSS, you'll be amazed when mysterious Rex Barrington III is unmasked in *I Married the Boss!* by Laura Anthony. In this month's FABULOUS FATHERS offering by Donna Clayton, a woman discovers *His Ten-Year-Old Secret.* And opposites attract in *The Rancher and the Heiress,* the third of Susan Meier's TEXAS FAMILY TIES miniseries.

WRANGLERS & LACE returns with Julianna Morris's *The Marriage Stampede.* In this appealing story, a cowgirl butts heads—and hearts—with a bachelor bent on staying that way. Sally Carleen unveils the first book in her exciting duo ON THE WAY TO A WEDDING… with the tale of a twin mistaken for an M.D.'s *Bride in Waiting!* It's both a blessing and a dilemma for a single mother when she's confronted with an amnesiac *Husband Found,* this month's FAMILY MATTERS title by Martha Shields.

Enjoy the timeless power of Romance this month, and every month—you won't be disappointed!

Mary-Theresa Hussey

Mary-Theresa Hussey
Senior Editor, Silhouette Romance

Please address questions and book requests to:
Silhouette Reader Service
U.S.: 3010 Walden Ave., P.O. Box 1325, Buffalo, NY 14269
Canadian: P.O. Box 609, Fort Erie, Ont. L2A 5X3

HIS TEN-YEAR-OLD SECRET

Donna Clayton

Silhouette
ROMANCE™
Published by Silhouette Books
America's Publisher of Contemporary Romance

With love to my brother-in-law,
Chip Fasano.
See, Chip, mechanics make great heroes!

And many thanks to Terry S. Greer,
the hot-rod information man.

SILHOUETTE BOOKS

ISBN 0-373-19373-4

HIS TEN-YEAR-OLD SECRET

This edition published by arrangement with Harlequin Books S.A.

® and TM are trademarks of Harlequin Books S.A., used under license. Trademarks indicated with ® are registered in the United States Patent and Trademark Office, the Canadian Trade Marks Office and in other countries.

Look us up on-line at: http://www.romance.net

Printed in U.S.A.

Books by Donna Clayton

Silhouette Romance

Mountain Laurel #720
Taking Love in Stride #781
Return of the Runaway Bride #999
Wife for a While #1039
Nanny and the Professor #1066
Fortune's Bride #1118
Daddy Down the Aisle #1162
*Miss Maxwell Becomes a Mom #1211
*Nanny in the Nick of Time #1217
*Beauty and the Bachelor Dad #1223
†The Stand-By Significant Other #1284
†Who's the Father of Jenny's Baby? #1302
The Boss and the Beauty #1342
His Ten-Year-Old Secret #1373

*The Single Daddy Club
†Mother & Child

DONNA CLAYTON

is proud to be a recipient of the Holt Medallion, an award honoring outstanding literary talent, for her Silhouette Romance novel *Wife for a While*. And seeing her work appear on the Waldenbooks Series bestsellers list has given her a great deal of joy and satisfaction.

Reading is one of Donna's favorite ways to while away a rainy afternoon. She loves to hike, too. Another hobby added to her list of fun things to do is traveling. She fell in love with Europe during her first trip abroad recently, and plans to return often. Oh, and Donna still collects cookbooks, but as her writing career grows, she finds herself using them less and less.

Donna loves to hear from her readers. Please write to her in care of Silhouette Books, 300 East 42nd Street, New York, NY 10017.

Fabulous Fathers

Dear Erin,

Please forgive your old dad for being sappy, but I need to tell you that—even with your grimy knees and elbows, and your ever-present baseball cap—I couldn't have been blessed with a more charming, beautiful and loving daughter. For almost ten years now, you and I have been on our own. We've had some lean times, you and I, but so far we've made it through. And I wouldn't change a day of the past.

I'm telling you all this for a reason. Your mom is back in town, and our lives are about to change forever. Tess Galloway had an unforgettable effect on my life once. And there's a pretty good chance that's not going to change this time around. But now you're involved. So I'm not afraid to tell you, I'm more than a little nervous about her arrival in Pine Meadow.

But the fact that your mom is here and eager to meet you has had me thinking about the kind of dad I've been. You and I tinkered with car engines when we should have been finding a teacher for piano lessons or visiting fancy museums. I may not have risen as far in the world as some people thought I should, I may only be a mechanic, but I'm your dad. I'll always be your dad. And I'll always love you with all my heart.

Love,

Dad

Prologue

She simply could not put off this chore any longer. Tess Galloway stood at the threshold of her father's bedroom door. The late-afternoon sun slanted golden through the window, casting streaks of light across the worn, brown rug. Absently Tess worried her bottom lip between her teeth and went inside.

The air still held a whispery trace of familiar spicy aftershave. Barely noticeable after all these weeks, the scent offered her a vague sense of comfort as she inhaled it deeply into her lungs, yet her heart pinched in her chest with painful longing.

The dark-stained pine of the bed's footboard was scarred and dull with age, the mattress sagging in the middle. Tess grinned gently at the memory of how her father had allowed her an occasional, albeit short, bed-jumping session when she'd been a little girl. She grazed her fingertips lightly across the cotton spread.

Two small steps had her standing in front of his bureau, and without even picking up the pipe that rested there, Tess detected the faint aroma of tobacco. The rich fragrance kindled feelings of deep love and total security the likes of which she would never again experience.

"Daddy," Tess whispered to the empty room. Her eyes stung as unexpected tears shattered her sight into glittering shards. "Oh, how I miss you."

A month had passed since Harry Galloway's funeral. For weeks Tess had found one excuse after another to keep from sorting through his belongings, packing up his clothes, cleaning out his bedroom.

But the chill of fall was in the air and close on its heels would be winter. She was certain there was someone in need of warm clothing. Her father's gray wool overcoat might be a bit frayed at the cuffs, but it would certainly keep someone toasty when the temperatures dipped low. And his olive mackintosh was just as rain repellent as ever. There were several suits. Trousers and a sport coat or two. Dress shirts and ties. Not to mention shoes. Three pair to be exact, all in good condition, seeing as how her father worked all his life in one shoe repair shop or another. It would be a sin to let such serviceable clothing hang in the closet, sit in the drawers, unused.

Tess dashed a tear trail from her cheek with the back of her hand. "This simply must be done," she told herself, giving the words an insistent inflection. "Today."

The topmost bureau drawer slid open and Tess dived into it with both hands, scooping out paired socks that had been rolled into balls and stragglers that had no mate but that her father hadn't been able to get rid of. There were neatly folded handkerchiefs, at least a dozen of them, one of which her dad slid into his back pocket every day. Harry Galloway would never have been caught without his trusty handkerchief. One never knew when one's glasses would need a good cleaning, or a park bench brushed off, or a little girl's nose wiped...

Again, Tess felt an achy spasm shoot through her chest.

"We're thick as thieves, me and you, Tessie." She could almost hear his soft, gentle voice as he'd described their close and loving relationship. Her dad had been an emotional man. Yes, he had.

She sniffed back another tear. "Stop, darn it," she chastised herself aloud.

Aggravated with herself, Tess pulled the second drawer completely free and dumped its contents onto the bed. V-necked T-shirts and cotton boxers tumbled into a pile. The third drawer held polo shirts and sweaters. One shabby-looking sweatshirt caught her eye and she picked it up. The pilled fabric was soft against her cheek and she remembered this was her father's favorite. The one he wore to work around the house. She set it aside. A cherished keepsake.

She found several pairs of shorts in the fourth drawer, and as she tossed them into the pile, she noticed they were threadbare in places. How few of them there were wasn't lost on her, either. Tess had been aware that her father had gone without for her. Boy, had she been aware.

He'd worked so hard. Had sacrificed so much. Just so she could earn the title of *Dr.* Tess Galloway. His greatest wish had been to provide her with a college and medical school education free from the strangling claws of bank loans. For several years he'd been successful, paying for her tuition and books with his meager salary, but not without a great deal of personal sacrifice. Because of Tess, Harry Galloway never took a vacation, never bought a new car and just simply made do with what he had or could acquire second-hand.

Not wanting the pile of her father's clothing to become so large it rolled to the floor, she stopped clearing out drawers and began to gently, lovingly tuck the clothing into a large plastic bag.

Her protests against all his sacrifice had fallen on deaf ears. Harry hadn't allowed Tess to work anything more than a part-time job all through her college years.

But as the tuition increased, and his salary hadn't, Harry was forced to allow Tess to seek out education loans through the University of Connecticut; however, he'd done everything he could to keep those debts to a minimum.

Tess had just finished her medical residency and had accepted a partnership in a large family practice. Her loans were almost miniscule compared to some of her graduating peers, and she was in a much better position than they would be for years to come. All due to her father's ceaseless efforts to pay the tuition bills, all due to his endless determination to set aside his own needs to provide for those of his daughter.

Once the bed was clear, she turned back to the bureau and bent to pull out the final drawer. A thought struck her with such startling suddenness that her spine straightened almost of its own accord, and she rested her hand on the bureau top.

With the smell of her father's pipe tobacco wafting around her, she realized that with all his making do, with all his self-sacrifice, he'd never once over the years made her feel the least bit guilty. He'd never made one comment to make her feel beholden. Never said a word meant to incite her need to feel obligated or indebted to him. He'd never once brought up her mistakes of the past. He'd simply given to her. He'd simply loved her. Unselfishly. Unconditionally.

He'd been such a kind, caring, *loving* parent.

With a sigh, Tess returned to the task at hand. She tugged the final, bottommost drawer from its slot and twisted toward the bed. Sweatpants and heavy work trousers fell out along with something that made a heavy *clunk* as it bounced onto the mattress.

Curiosity knit her brow as she brushed aside one leg of a pair of navy sweatpants to see the object more clearly.

It was a box. A tin box. A tad smaller than a shoe box. The blue paint had chipped away in several places allowing rust to eat at the metal.

The edge of the mattress depressed as Tess sat down. She picked up the box, acutely aware of the coolness of its surface. The latch caught, and for a moment she thought the box was locked. But the latch finally gave, and the lid sprang free.

Envelopes, a tight bundle of them, were crammed in the tight space. A rubber band secured them together. These weren't regular white letter envelopes. They looked official. No, they looked like oversize, tan *business* envelopes. And they were unopened. Tess had to strain to pry them out of the cramped space. There looked to be over a hundred of them. However, before she was able to examine them too closely, her attention was caught by the small book resting in the bottom of the box. The tiny book's rough, black cover was reminiscent of the old register books banks gave out before the age of computerized accounts. Utter bewilderment had her head shaking back and forth as she wondered what in the world she'd discovered.

After setting the envelopes aside, Tess picked up the bankbook, turned it over and her mouth opened in surprise, but no sound came forth.

Minster Savings And Loan, Pine Meadow, N.J.

Walloped with an overwhelming wave of weakness, she was relieved to be sitting because her whole body felt suddenly shaky. That name. Minster. It hadn't been mentioned between her and her father in...*years*.

Seldom did Tess allow herself to even think it, because doing so only stirred up memories. Haunting memories of a love she'd felt so strongly the mere thought of it was enough to swallow her whole. But when she did indulge herself, when she did permit herself to get lost in remembering, she did so only in the very deepest part of the night, when there was no chance of her reminiscence being discovered.

However, the Minster name also conjured in her an ache. A terrible ache caused by a loss so complete it had left a hole in her life that would never be filled.

With well-practiced determination, she shoved the tormenting memory aside. It was either that, or risk getting completely caught up in the past.

She focused on the tin box instead. What did it mean, this old account book? These unopened bank statements?

Her fingers trembled as she cracked open the spine of the small black book. The balance scrawled on the yellowed page made her gasp aloud.

Chapter One

"Sounds like Ol' Lady Warrington let that hairy rat she calls a dog crawl up into this engine."

Dylan Minster listened intently to the rough idle of the sweet, old Cadillac, his eyes riveted to the running engine.

"The first thing we need to do," he said over the engine noise, "is pop off the distributor cap. Make sure it's clean. No cracks."

His daughter knew this already, he was sure. She was nearly ten years old now, and she'd been working on cars with him since she was a babe in diapers. But it never hurt to reiterate.

"Hand me a flathead screwdriver, Erin."

The tool that was slapped into his palm didn't have a flat, smooth head, but the crisscrossed one of a Phillips. He grinned. He had Erin now. This mistake was downright silly and deserved at least an hour's worth of teasing. And he'd gladly oblige.

"You're in for it now," he said. But when he

swung around expecting to see Erin, he came face-to-face with his stern-eyed mother.

When she offered him no greeting, he said, "Hi, Ma. How are you?"

"First of all," she told him, "I take offense for poor Edith Warrington. She is *not* an old lady..."

"Aww, now." He grinned, hoping to soften her obvious disapproval. "I didn't mean any harm."

"*And* Corky is a lovely little long-haired terrier," she went on. "Not 'a hairy rat.' Edith is a wonderful friend. And she loves that dog like a baby. If she ever heard you talk like that—"

"She's not going to hear me talk like that, Ma," Dylan assured his mother.

"The only reason Edith patronizes your shop—" her gaze skirted loathsomely around the cluttered bay "—is because you are my son, and—"

"I know, Ma." Dylan's smile dissolved. His mother had a way of making that happen quite often. "And I appreciate the business your name brings me."

"It's your name, too."

If only you'd do something with it. Her blatant motherly advice echoed unspoken in the air. He chose to ignore it.

Helen Minster tipped up her chin. And Dylan got the distinct impression that, now that she'd had her say, the subject was closed. He sighed.

"So what brings you out this afternoon?" he asked.

He watched his mother glance over her shoulder at her granddaughter who sat behind the steering wheel of Edith Warrington's old Caddy.

She turned back to face him. "Why isn't missy there in school?"

"Her name's Erin, Ma," he said quietly.

"Look at her," Helen continued. "She's filthy. Her hair's a mess. Her fingernails are greasy. And she's—"

"Ma." His voice was clipped just enough to make her stop. "Let's talk about this in my office." Giving his daughter a quick glance, he said, "Cut the engine, hon. I'll be right back."

He stalked off toward the side door leading to his office, making every effort to dampen the burning embers of his anger.

Dylan was well aware of the fact that he was his mother's worst and only disappointment. That he was no comparison to his brother and sister, both shining examples of the education, polish and success that Minster money could buy. And because he knew all these things, took full responsibility for them, he tried hard to be patient with her.

Flipping on the light in his small office, Dylan felt a self-conscious tweak as he looked around at the shabby furniture. The sorry excuse he called a desk was beat-up, the heavy gray metal dented and scratched. The couch was propped up on one corner by a red brick. And the leather seat of his desk chair was cracked in several places.

Funny how he never seemed to notice how neglected his surroundings were until his mother came to visit. Which, thankfully, was only on rare occasions.

"Have a seat," he told her, rounding his desk and easing himself down onto his chair.

She eyed the couch distastefully. "I don't mind standing, thank you."

"Suit yourself." He snatched up a pen from the desktop, squeezing it between his thumb and index finger. "Erin had a headache this morning," he explained. "She came to work with me and took a nap in my office. She woke up feeling better, so she was helping me out in the shop."

"Well, when she woke up feeling better," his mother stated, "you should have taken her to school."

"Ma—" Dylan's shoulder sagged with the effort of this justification, but he was so used to this kind of interrogation that he barely noticed. "It's after two o'clock. She'd have been in school an hour." Then a thought occurred to him. "How did you know Erin wasn't in school today?"

Helen Minster's lips pursed for an instant. Then she said, "If you must know, I asked the school secretary to call me if Erin was absent."

Patience, Dylan reminded himself. He asked softly, "Why would you do a thing like that?"

"Dylan, this is a new school year. Erin *must* start off on the right foot." She shifted the position of the purse handle that hung on her forearm. "I don't know why you won't allow me to send the child to boarding school. I sent you to boarding school." She paused, as if she had second thoughts about the statement, eyeing him pointedly.

And just look what you did with the education I provided for you.

His mother's accusation couldn't have been clearer if she'd said it out loud.

Then she added, "As well as your brother and sister."

"Public school is fine for Erin, Ma," he told her. "All Erin's friends attend the school here in Pine Meadow. She'd be miserable if she had to go to a new school. She's getting a fine education right where she is."

He didn't want his daughter feeling as lonely and out of place as he had felt as a youngster being shipped off to boarding school. He hated every moment he'd been away from Pine Meadow and his friends and family. However, he'd bent to his mother's will because as a child he'd had no other choice. Until high school, anyway, when he'd discovered that a threatened expulsion due to fistfighting with his classmates was the perfect way to force her to let him attend school in his hometown.

"Yes," his mother said, "and she's getting that education along with every piece of riffraff Pine Meadow has to offer."

"You know my views on that subject," Dylan said wearily. "Erin's going to be dealing with all kinds of people as an adult. Black, white, yellow, brown, rich and poor. It'll do her good to learn to get along with everyone while she's a kid."

"Humph, maybe." Helen Minster was obviously unconvinced. Then her eyes lit with a new attack. "But boarding school would get her away from this place. And it's this grease pit I most want to get her away from. She should be taking piano lessons, or ballet lessons. She should be reading *Black Beauty* and *Little Women.* That child should be wearing lacy dresses and patent leather shoes."

She stopped suddenly, hesitating long enough to take a deep breath, get herself under control

"Dylan, that child is soon going to be ten years old. She's a young lady now. She shouldn't be tinkering underneath the hood of a car, her hands filthy with grease. This…this *mechanic shop*—" she said the two words as if they were knives that stabbed her "—isn't any place for a young lady. It isn't right that you're allowing Erin to follow you around like some oily little monkey whose only goal in life is to hand her daddy a screwdriver or a socket wrench.''

Up until now, he'd been resting his chin on his fist. But the moment his mother had called his daughter a greasy primate, he'd had to clamp his fingers over his mouth, his thumb planted firmly under his jaw to keep from growling at her to get the hell out of his office, out of his shop.

She's only trying to help, he chanted in his head. *She only wants what's best for her granddaughter.*

He looked out the window that separated his office from the three work bays that made up the shop. Erin had her head stuck under the hood of the car parked in the first bay. The bill of her baseball cap was twisted to the back of her head. Her elbows and knees were nut brown with grime, her denim shorts and cotton top smeared and grubby as well. His heart hitched in his chest. That little girl was his whole life. His whole world.

''That child needs some feminine influence,'' Helen said. ''And if she doesn't get it soon, it's going to be too late. You mark my words.''

Too late for what? Dylan was too preoccupied to ask. He was too busy wondering if his mother might be right. Was he doing Erin a great disservice by allowing her to spend time at the shop? Should he be chauffeuring her around to piano lessons and ballet recitals rather than teaching her how to change an engine's spark plugs and fuel filter?

''I think you ought to let Erin move in with me,'' Helen said.

His knee-jerk reaction was to say, ''No way.'' But the response fell on deaf ears.

"I can teach her to be a proper young lady," his mother argued. "You do want her to grow up into a woman who can hold her head up in this town, don't you? You do want her to be proud of who she is? Do you think that's going to happen when she spends most of her life—" she looked around again, disdain evident in every muscle of her face "—hanging around *Dylan's Auto Repair?*"

Usually he wasn't at all fazed by the disgust his mother showed when she spoke the name of his business. Usually he allowed her disappointment in him to roll off him like water off a rain slicker. Usually. But today it struck him—like a forceful, unexpected poke in the gut with a tire iron.

"You think about it," his mother said. "And when you do, I want you to consider long and hard what's best for Erin. Not what's best for you."

She opened the door of his office then, and carefully picked her way through the dirty clutter of car parts toward the big open door of the garage bay, taking care not to allow the hem of her yellow dress to become soiled. Helen Minster called a curt goodbye to her granddaughter and then disappeared from his view.

Almost immediately, Erin was standing in the threshold of his office. "You okay, Dad?"

He nodded. "Sure, hon," he told her. "Give me a few minutes, okay?"

She smiled and then went back to fiddling with the Caddy's engine.

Dylan sat at his desk for a long time, studying her. Tendrils of wavy red hair escaped from under the cap on her head. Concentration creased her brow as she searched in the large metal box for some tool or other.

The love he felt for that little girl out there was so

great it actually made his chest ache. And he found it more than a little worrisome to think that letting her hang out here at the shop with him might be harming her in some way.

Okay, he thought, so we have a problem. His daughter's femininity needed a little...fine-tuning. Hell, he told himself, tell the truth, Erin's feminine side needed a complete overhaul!

As much as he hated to admit it, his mother was probably right. Erin should be reading great works of literature. She should be involved in culturally enriching activities. And there couldn't possibly be a less likely place for a little girl to find polish and refinement than an auto repair shop.

He stroked his chin over and over between his index finger and thumb as his mind churned. Boarding school was out of the question in his mind. But was the solution packing Erin off to live in Minster House with his mother?

"Over my dead body," he whispered too low for anyone but himself to hear.

Pine Meadow certainly hadn't changed much in the ten years she'd been away, Tess mused as she drove through town. Certainly, the strip mall on the main thoroughfare was new, or at least new to her, as the shops had looked well established when she'd passed by them. But the First Methodist Church looked the same as ever. As did the supermarket on the corner of Main and North Streets. And the fact that the billboard hovering over the double doors of the Main Street Theater advertised Hollywood's hottest movie let her know the cinema was still doing a booming business. Tess had spent many a Saturday afternoon in the cool, dark recesses of that movie house while her father was busy at his shop. And then as a teen, her theater visits changed to Saturday *nights*. When she'd sneaked out on dates with Dylan Minster.

His name whispered across her mind, across her thoughts, sending shivers skittering across her skin.

Lord, how she had loved him. And the things she'd learned from him...

Tenderness. Commitment. Affection. *Passion.*

The closeness and devotion they had shared together rivaled even that between Shakespeare's infamous Romeo and Juliet.

Tess smiled. The childishly fanciful manner in which she thought of her relationship with Dylan was inevitable, entirely natural, she guessed, seeing as how she'd been so young when they'd been a couple. Her smile faded, though, because along with tender passion, he'd taught her other things as well.

Pain. And guilt. And anger.

The awful names he'd called her had the flush of humiliation rushing to her face even after all this time. It was so sad that the three wonderful years they spent together were marred forever by the one hostile, accusation-filled fight they'd had. The fight that had her finally agreeing to leave Pine Meadow with her father. The hateful words Dylan had used as weapons to assault her had been a devastating turning point in her life. Without them, without hearing Dylan's opinion of her face-to-face, she'd have never left New Jersey with her father. She'd have never run away from the young man who had captured her heart so completely. No matter the threats from his well-respected and wealthy family. No matter the consequences.

Braking for a red light, she forced herself to rise

from the foggy haze of her memories. She'd automatically switched on her left turn signal, and as she waited for the light to change, she realized she was staring at the red brick building that had always been the home of Minster Savings and Loan.

Fear welled up inside her seemingly out of nowhere. A fear so pure, so unadulterated, it had her heart pounding, her blood whooshing in her eardrums. It mattered not one whit that the panic threatening to drown her was irrational. The fact that Helen Minster, or the rest of the Minster clan, could no longer hurt her was too logical a thought; besides, it was buried under about a dump truck load of frantic insanity that had perspiration prickling her underarms and her brain screaming at her to get the hell out of this town, get the hell away from the prejudice of the judgmental Minsters. Such thinking caused nothing but heartache, humiliation and hurt for people like herself.

She'd worked so hard not to obsess about the account book she'd found among her father's possessions. But now questions and conclusions swam in her head until she thought she'd surely drown in them.

Had her father accepted some kind of payoff from Helen Minster? There really was no other explanation that Tess could come up with. Had they really been paid to leave Pine Meadow? She shook her head, thinking the only possible answer to that was yes. And all this time Tess had been under the impression she and her father had left town of their own free will, with their chins held high, their pride intact. But it seemed their exodus had been under a whole different set of circumstances entirely. But if what she surmised was true, why hadn't her father used that money when the two of them had been in such need of it over the years? The interest had accrued on that account, and not one dime had ever been withdrawn. That didn't seem to make sense, and it was that part of the situation that had her curious for answers. It was that part of the situation that had compelled Tess to take a leave of absence from her new practice and travel to Pine Meadow.

She had to admit, there was one question that haunted her more than any other. Had Dylan been aware of the payoff?

A horn blared behind her and she stomped her foot on the gas pedal, desperate to get away from the bank and all the mocking questions it conjured. Her tires screeched a complaint as she took the turn much too quickly. Another turn had her heading toward Pine Meadow's east end. The "Bowers," as the area had been known years ago. The wrong side of the tracks. The bad part of town. *Her* part of town.

She slowed the car and gulped in several deep breaths in an effort to calm her troubled mind. Being back in her neck of the woods, seeing her old haunts, somehow comforted her. And she focused all her attention on them, the narrow streets and close-packed businesses soothing her frazzled nerves.

Home. The businesses in the Bowers had been mostly small, family-owned enterprises that struggled from month to month to remain open. These people had known no other way of life. Had no other means to eke out a living. And from the looks of things, that hadn't changed.

She turned down Cox Avenue and slowed down when she came to the building her father used to rent as his shoe repair shop. The main floor of the small building housed a coffee shop now. And seeing the frilly, faded yellow curtains hanging in the two up-stairs windows, she surmised that someone lived in the tiny one bedroom apartment where she had been raised.

Heaving a forlorn sigh, she continued driving down the street. She'd played hopscotch on this sidewalk as a little girl. Jumped rope with her friends. Tess wrapped herself in the warm blanketlike memory of the love and security she'd felt as a child. Looking both ways at the four-way stop, that's when she saw it.

Dylan's Auto Repair.

The small, metal placard advertising Body Work dangled from below the Auto Repair sign, as if it had been added on. A second thought.

Could it be…?

"No," came her verbal reply. Dylan Minster's favorite hobby might have been working on cars, but he'd made it abundantly clear that he was going into his family's banking business. Abundantly clear. Besides, a Minster would never be caught dead opening a business in the Bowers.

Still, her eyes remained glued to that sign. It seemed to call out to her. Relentless. Enticing. Like a glass of cool water to someone dying of thirst.

"Hey, there!"

Tess's gaze whipped around to see an elderly lady standing on the corner.

"You lost?" she asked.

"Oh, no," Tess told her. "I grew up around here. Lived overtop the coffee shop a couple of blocks back. My dad had a shoe repair shop there."

"Well, now." The woman smiled. "I don't remember the shop being anything other than a coffeehouse.

But I've only lived here seven years. Ever since I had to move in with my daughter and her husband.'' Her smile widened. ''Welcome home.''

''Thanks.'' Tess's tone was vague as her eyes were inexorably drawn back to the auto repair shop. Then she found herself saying, ''Things haven't changed too much.'' She paused. ''But I see there are a few new businesses in the Bowers...''

The hesitation had been purposeful. Tess hoped the woman would reveal some information regarding the garage across the street.

The woman chuckled. ''The city council has tried every way possible to get people to stop calling this place the Bowers. They started a campaign a few years back. Wanted us to call this part of town East Meadows. That fell flat. People use what they know, I guess. And this place will always be the Bowers, won't it?''

''I guess,'' Tess said, her gaze never leaving the building she'd hoped to learn more about.

Finally the woman seemed to perceive her interest. ''You know Dylan Minster?''

After several moments Tess was able to get her tongue to work. ''I did. Once. A long time ago.'' The curt sentences sounded rusty to her own ears.

''That Dylan fought his family, the city council and a whole army of other people when he wanted to open his garage over here.''

By *over here,* Tess knew she meant in this less reputable part of town.

Movement caught her eye, and then she saw him. He stood in the large open doorway of the first bay, directing as someone backed a large car out of the garage. Tess felt every nerve ending in her body come alive, alert.

Dylan Minster. In the flesh. She'd know the set of those wide, muscular shoulders anywhere, recognize the tilt of that chin. That was the man who had stolen her heart. The man who had taught her what love between two people was all about. However, he was also the man who had crushed her spirit, hurt her like no one else ever had. The man who had fathered her stillborn baby girl. Her gaze never wavered from his fine form as her mind churned with all these bits from the past.

"You know," the woman said to her, "seeing as how you knew Dylan and all, and seeing as how you're in the neighborhood, you ought to stop in over there and say hello."

Tess's voice actually quivered as she answered, "I think I'll do that."

Chapter Two

The broad expanse of his chest made the navy, run-of-the-mill uniform shirt look not quite so run-of-the-mill. The rolled-up sleeves revealed powerful, tanned hands and forearms, the open collar, a corded neck that invited a woman's lips to explore.

Tess started with a tiny twitch, her eyes widening. Where had that thought come from?

From the deepest depths of your memory, came a silent answer. *That most sensuous of places that Dylan had awakened when you were just seventeen.*

Well, she decided, such thoughts would simply have to go straight back to wherever they came from, and she'd have to shut the door on them. *Lock* the door on them. And toss away the key.

After checking the street traffic one more time, she inched across the intersection and then steered toward the asphalt parking lot of the garage.

She stopped the car, its engine idling softly. "Are you out of your mind?" she whispered to herself.

"What are you doing?" Did she really believe Dylan would want to see her after all this time? After all the mean words they had hurled at each other?

But that seemed like a lifetime ago. They were both adults now, weren't they?

She cringed at the question, remembering how very grown-up she'd thought she'd been at seventeen. Seventeen and pregnant.

Again, she brushed her memories of the past aside, turning the key to cut the engine. There were questions that needed answers. She really didn't care one way or the other if Dylan would *want* to see her. He was going to see her.

Tess got out of her car, but it was the sound of her car door closing that had him looking her way. He called out for the driver of the big, white Cadillac to stop, and the car halted with a slight jerk.

His dark head tilted the tiniest bit and those deep green eyes of his narrowed, a frown creasing his brow.

She stopped about ten feet from him. A buffer zone of sorts.

"Hello, Dylan," she said, reaching up and pulling off her sunglasses.

His gaze widened with recognition when she spoke, almost as though he'd known who she was, but refused to believe it until she actually addressed him. A dozen wild gypsies stomped out a boisterous jig on her nerves as she awaited his response.

Ho-ly hell! Tess. Tess Galloway. How she'd changed!

The teenage girl who had knocked him out of his high-top basketball sneakers all those years ago had been rail-thin, the sprinkling of freckles across her nose and cheeks irresistible to him then.

Apparently the coltish Tess had grown up. Her girlish figure had filled out with the kind of womanly curves that fueled a man's dreams when he was asleep and vulnerable. And not a single freckle could be found on her pale-as-moonlight complexion. Her manicured nails told him she'd broken the childish proclivity of nibbling on them when she was worried. Remembering how she'd lamented, again and again, what she'd thought was an unbreakable habit, he nearly smiled. Nearly. But he successfully reined it in.

But one thing about her hadn't changed. Her eyes. Brown as rich, dark chocolate, and just as luscious.

That gaze alone was enough to have his libido churning down low in his gut. But put together the whole package, the angelic face, the bewitching curves, and no man was safe against a gnawing hunger that had nothing to do with food. The grown-up Tess Galloway would tweak the sexual appetite of any man.

Reaching into his back pocket with as much nonchalance as he could muster, he pulled out an oily old rag. He wiped at the grease on his forearm and said, ''Well, well, well.''

Immediately he bit down on a silent groan. For years he'd practiced what he'd say if Tess were ever to show up in his life again. He'd filled a multitude of aching, need-filled nights imagining this moment, coming up with witty, double entendres meant to show her how great he was doing without her and make her regret leaving Pine Meadow, leaving *him*. But what had just come out of his mouth couldn't have sounded more lame.

Absently he stuffed the rag into his back pocket. "Look what just blew in with the wind."

Oh, Lord. He was going from bad to worse.

It was this damned surge of testosterone, he knew. The rush of hormones was hogging his body's blood flow, making it impossible for his brain, or his tongue, to function properly.

Enough! the logical part of his mind cut in like a razor-edged knife. Why the hell are you lusting after this woman? Isn't she the one who left you all alone? Isn't she the one who sent Erin to you with an attitude so casual, so blasé, it seemed to say she thought their child was like some stray mutt that needed tending?

His jaw clenched tight. Good. Anger. Strong enough to sink his teeth into. Strong enough to suffocate the desire burning a hole deep in his belly.

Like a flurry of sharp blows to his chin, memories bombarded him. Erin, crying with diaper rash, and he, a new father who knew zip about a cure. Erin, sick and weepy with a high fever. Erin, demanding attention when he was nothing but dog tired after a long day at work.

Excellent, he thought. He wanted to recall all the bad experiences he'd had as a single father. He urged those fearful, nerve-racking, irritating memories forward, in fact. They would be the perfect stones and mortar to build himself a sturdy wall of defense against the woman standing in front of him.

"So—" he heard the clipped edge in his tone and liked it, latched onto it, actually, as if it was some kind of weapon with the ability to protect him "—you've finally come to see how your little puppy dog has fared after all these years."

A light autumn breeze blew a few wayward strands

of her glorious red hair into her face and she shoved them back with her free hand, her long nails combing through the tresses with one smooth stroke. Only when her face was free from obstruction did he see the bewilderment knitting her brow, clouding those gorgeous mahogany eyes.

"My little…"

Her words faded as she stopped to moisten her lips, and the sight of her delicate pink tongue sent his heart hammering his ribs like the pistons of a prime, ass-kicking, 100-horse-power engine. Why had time turned her into such a beautiful and elegant swan?

Not that she'd been an ugly duckling as a teen. No stretch of the imagination could have him saying that. Hell, she'd been cute as a damn kitten. He was reminded just how cute she'd been every time he looked at Erin—Tess's spitting image. But the years that had passed had made the woman in front of him far more than merely attractive. She was a radiant, dazzling diamond.

Suddenly he blinked. Was that pain he read in her gaze? What the hell did she have to feel hurt about?

"I never thought of you like that, Dylan," she said softly. "I never did."

Rage flashed red before his eyes like leaping flames.

"Me?" he snarled. "I'm not talking about *me*."

The frown in her brow bit deeper, but he was so infuriated he couldn't be bothered giving it a second thought.

"I'm talking about the little stray you so heartlessly sent back to me," he ranted on quietly. "The waif you thought was so useless you didn't even give her a name before you got rid of her."

"I'm—"

Dylan watched her head shake, her hand raise to splay at the base of her throat.

"I, ah, I don't under—"

Erin chose that very moment to shut off the engine, open the heavy door of the Caddy and get out of the car. Glancing back over his shoulder, he was grateful to see that the car's windows had been closed. Maybe the noise of the idling engine had kept his daughter from hearing what he'd said. Lord, he hoped so. The last thing he wanted was for Erin's self-esteem to be injured by thinking she hadn't been wanted. Although that *was* the fact of the matter—at least from Tess's side of things.

"Daa-aad." Erin drew out the word as only an eager, impatient kid could. "You said I could park Mrs. Warrington's Caddy. Please don't change your mind. I already got it halfway out the door and I didn't hit nothin' yet."

"You didn't hit *anything* yet." This probably wasn't the best time to correct Erin's grammar, but the action was automatic. Besides, he couldn't have his daughter speaking like a heathen, now, could he?

Erin must have realized they weren't alone because she grew quiet and came to stand beside him.

"Hi," she said to Tess, offering a friendly smile. "My name's Erin. Erin Minster. How are ya today?"

The daddy in Dylan couldn't help but feel a prideful tug inside. Erin had never had a problem with shyness, that was for sure, and he'd taught her that amiability was a great way to secure the return business of customers.

Tess didn't respond, but that didn't stop Erin. "You having car trouble?" the child tried again. "You've come to the right place, 'cause my dad can fix anything that runs on gasoline.''

He indulged himself in just looking at his marvellous little girl who never ceased to cause a fuzzy, satisfied warmth to flow through him that only a "hand's on" kind of dad could feel. But his smile faded as he glanced back at Tess.

His mouth firmed into a fine line as he noticed her expression was nothing short of...earth-shattering.

Well what in heaven's name had Tess expected? A baby? Coming into town ten years after the child's birth, of course their daughter was going to be all grown up. A young lady, as his mother had described Erin earlier. Had Tess anticipated meeting a toddler or something? Why did she look so astounded?

Tess's brown eyes seemed to churn with storm clouds as she studied Erin. When she lifted her gaze to his, it was filled with silent, thunderous questions he found quite bewildering. Then her attention clamped once again on their daughter.

Finally she uttered a soft, breathy, "Oh, my," turned on her heel and raced toward her car. In another moment, she was speeding away.

"Wow," Erin said to him when the wheel-flung pebbles in the parking lot settled. "What was *her* problem?"

Dylan didn't answer. Not because he meant to ignore his daughter's query, but because he didn't quite know what to say.

It wasn't his fault that Tess Galloway was having trouble facing her daughter. It wasn't his fault she couldn't cope with what she'd done in the past. And it wasn't his fault she felt the need to once again flee from her responsibility.

However, his silence was more telling than he'd realized.

"You know her, don't you, Dad?"

All he could do was look down into Erin's chocolate-brown gaze.

"So, who is she?" Erin asked, already sensing the answer to her first question.

Heaving a weary sigh, Dylan debated what to say. How to answer. He could lie. Tell the child he had no idea who the crazy woman was. But Tess Galloway would probably be back. Of course, it was entirely possible that she'd run away again, just as she'd done before, and he and Erin would never see hide nor hair of her. But she certainly wouldn't leave town before causing him as much trouble as she could. That was about how his luck ran. However, he refused to allow Tess to damage the trust he knew his daughter placed in him, so telling the child the truth and helping her deal with it was probably the best path to follow.

"That," he said with a slow, measured reluctance, "was your mother."

The faint odor of cigarette smoke hanging in the still air was plain evidence that the hotel clerk had made a mistake in booking Tess's room. She'd specified a smoke-free room. But the idea was so small it was meaningless when weighed against the gargantuan revelation that had her in complete and utter turmoil.

She paced the seven steps it took to reach the far wall, then turned and paced back to the door of the tiny bathroom.

Her baby daughter hadn't died.

Her baby daughter hadn't died.

Raking all ten fingers through her hair, Tess paused

in front of the dressing mirror and stared at her reflection as she was lambasted with questions and ideas that seemed to fly at her like dive-bombing fighter planes.

How could this have happened? How could a woman give birth and...

She stopped the thought in midstream. She hadn't been a woman. She'd been a girl. A teenager. Still how could *any* female, of *any* age, give birth to a baby and not know that her daughter lived? Such a thing was inconceivable...wasn't it? Things like that didn't really happen. Those kind of situations were only impossible, unbelievable fictionalized ideas thought up by movie-of-the-week scriptwriters.

Things like this simply didn't happen to sane, rational, *normal* people like herself.

At the moment, though, Tess felt anything *but* sane and rational.

Erin.

Erin Minster.

Staring unblinkingly into the mirror, Tess saw an older version of the child's face. Erin had *her* eyes. Erin had *her* nose. *Her* mouth. *Her* chin. *Her* hair.

There was no doubt in her mind that Erin was her baby.

Her daughter was alive!

And Tess had run from her the instant she'd made the connection. Her eyes rolled upward and she closed her lids. Why had she made such a dash for her car? Why hadn't she simply stayed and talked things out with Dylan? Why hadn't she introduced herself to her daughter?

She had no other excuse except to say that the discovery had been staggering. No, it had been mind-blowing. A literal bombshell that had devastated her thinking processes.

Alive. And well. And living with her father in Pine Meadow.

How could this be? How could this have happened?

Worrying the small pearl pendant that hung on the delicate gold chain around her neck, Tess resumed her pacing.

Had Dylan somehow kidnapped Erin from the hospital in Connecticut where Tess had given birth?

She knew that Dylan had been rebellious in his youth, but she'd never witnessed him break the law. Besides, the idea that he might have abducted their child simply didn't make sense when she thought of the awful accusations he'd made when she'd come to him with the news of her pregnancy.

''You won't trap me into marriage,'' he'd railed at her.

His choice of hurtful words had clearly told her that he didn't want her. That he didn't want their baby. So she really couldn't imagine him turning around and stealing their child from the hospital nursery.

Furthermore, even if Dylan had been the type of person who could do such a thing, with doctors and nurses milling around, she just didn't think it would be easy to pull off. No matter what the movie-of-the-week scriptwriters might want TV watchers to believe.

But the Minsters were wealthy enough to pay off a doctor or nurse. The thought floated eerily into her mind, and she shivered.

People who chose to work in the medical profession did so to help people, not hurt them, she reminded herself. *Yes, but,* a tiny voice piped in, *there was al-*

ways someone who was desperate enough to act unethically. Especially if money was involved.

Suddenly Tess felt sick to her stomach to think the man she'd thought had been the love of her life would hurt her so terribly. Would rob her of her own flesh and blood.

He had been vicious when he broke up with you all those years ago, the tiny voice echoed in her head.

Yes, she remembered. He had been vicious.

She unwittingly nibbled the cuticle of one thumb. Why didn't things seem to add up? she wondered. Why didn't the pieces fit?

The scene at Dylan's garage earlier today unfolded again in her mind. All afternoon she'd been replaying the bit where Erin had come into the picture. Her gorgeous little girl had stepped out of the driver's seat as if she'd been born there. Tess couldn't help but smile.

However, she forced herself to push the endearing image aside and focus on what had happened *prior* to Erin's appearance. What had she said to Dylan? More importantly, what had he said to her?

"So," his words floated into her mind, *"you've finally come to see how your little puppy dog has fared after all these years."* Her breath caught as his meaning cut her to the quick. Then, she remembered him saying, *"I'm not talking about me. I'm talking about the little stray you so heartlessly sent back to me. The waif you thought was so useless you didn't even give her a name before you got rid of her."*

The realization was enough to make her knees buckle, and she sank onto the mattress, burying her face in her hands.

Dylan thought she hadn't wanted Erin. He thought she'd heartlessly sent her newborn daughter away without even giving the child a name. He thought she hadn't wanted to raise her own baby. He thought she'd known all along of her child's whereabouts, but that she hadn't even cared enough to call or visit or—

Tess groaned audibly. Dear Lord in heaven, Dylan had thought all these horrible things about her for the last ten years! She pressed trembling fingers against her mouth as one final, chilling question came to her.

What must her little girl think of her?

Without another thought, Tess grabbed her purse and headed for the door.

"The garage is closed."

Tess spun around to see the same elderly lady with whom she'd talked before, the same one who had urged her, only a couple of hours ago, to stop in and visit Dylan.

"Yes, I see that," Tess said, still wrestling with the disappointment she experienced over seeing the Closed sign hanging in the window of Dylan's place of business. She'd had the thought of going to Minster House to look for him, but didn't know if she had the nerve to do so. "The sign there says he opens at eight in the morning."

She hated the thought of waiting all those hours before having the chance to talk to Dylan. And Erin.

A thrill shot through her body with a jolt when she realized all over again that her baby was alive. Really alive!

"Eight, sharp," the woman said.

Defeat rounded Tess's shoulders. "I guess I'll come back tomorrow. Thanks for coming over to talk."

"*Aww,* now—" the woman actually seemed embarrassed "—there's no cause to go thanking me. Just trying to be neighborly. And seeing as how you sped out of here earlier like an arrow out of a bow, didn't seem like you and Dylan had much chance to catch up on things.''

''No.'' Now it was Tess's turn to feel chagrined. ''You're right, we didn't.'' But she simply couldn't bring herself to explain the situation.

What could she say? That she'd just discovered today that she has a daughter?

This woman would think she was a raving lunatic!

''Well, I'd better go find someplace to grab some dinner.'' The last thing Tess wanted was food. But she needed a means to politely take her leave. She had a hotel room floor that needed pacing, hours that needed worrying through. She turned away and started toward her car.

''You know...''

Something in the woman's tone made her jerk to a halt and spin around. The elderly lady's mouth was curled into a soft smile.

''I know how you can contact Dylan,'' she said. ''If you've a mind to, that is.''

Tess's silent, eager expression was answer enough to make the woman chuckle.

''You see, Dylan has his phone number listed there—'' she pointed to a small, index-card-size note taped in a lower corner of the window ''—just in case of an emergency. I had to call him once when a bunch of boys were hanging about in the parking lot here and getting up to no good.''

With her hopes soaring, Tess rushed to the window, scrambling in her purse for something to write with at the same time.

"Thank you," she told the woman. "Thank you so much."

She shrugged. "I didn't do you any favors. His number is there in the window for all the world to see."

Tess protested, "Yes, but—"

"Would you stop already," the woman said, grinning. "And go make your call. There's a telephone right there on the corner."

"I will." Tess stuffed the ink pen back into her purse and then began fishing for change as she headed for the phone booth.

Dylan answered on the third ring, the sound of his voice like a soft caress against Tess's ear.

"Dylan," she said, making every effort to speak smoothly, "it's Tess."

There were several seconds of dead silence.

Finally she heard him exhale in a short, puffy sort of sigh.

"I've got to admit," he said quietly, "you've surprised me again. I thought I might hear from you, but not quite so soon. How'd you get my home number?"

Not wanting to get the elderly lady who had helped her into hot water, Tess only told him half the truth. "From the emergency card you have posted in the front window at your auto repair shop."

"Ah."

The small sound was velvet soft over the phone line.

"And you thought this constituted an emergency."

Tess listened hard, but detected no censure in his tone, and she was left believing that this was his way of filling what would have otherwise been an awkward silence.

"It is to me," she told him. "We need to talk, Dylan."

Again, he sighed, but this one was tinged with irritation.

"Look," he said, "this isn't a good time. I'm trying to get dinner. And thanks to my mother, Erin has a boatload of make-up work that needs to be done before school tomorrow. It isn't a good time for you to be coming over here and disrupting Erin's life—"

"I have no intention of disrupting anything," Tess said, cutting in. It broke her heart to hear him talk of cooking dinner and helping with homework so mundanely when she'd never once had the opportunity to do such things for her daughter.

"Dylan…" The pleading in her voice was so thick, she had to stop.

All she wanted to do was make him understand. But if she were to simply blurt out the situation; that she'd been lied to, that she'd thought all these years that their baby was dead, that someone had committed a horrendous crime by stealing her child, he'd think she'd gone completely insane. She needed to see him face-to-face. She needed to tell him everything in a calm, rational manner. That was the only way to make him understand she was telling the truth.

Before she could speak, he said, "I want you to know that I won't allow you to upset Erin. I don't want you overwhelming her."

"I understand," she said. "I don't want to overwhelm her, either."

She'd never dream of causing her daughter one moment of worry or trouble.

"M-maybe," she stumbled over her thoughts as

they came at her, "it would be best if you and I met. Just to talk. To catch up."

The third sigh he expelled was weary sounding.

"I told you, Tess. I'm in the middle of fixing dinner. And then there's Erin's schoolwork. I want to be here if she needs me."

"Of course," she quickly agreed. "But maybe after? There's a coffee shop down the street from your garage. In the same building where my dad had his shop. We can talk there."

"It'll be at least two hours. And I don't know if I can find a sitter."

"I'll wait," she said in a rush.

She heard yet another exhalation.

"*Please,* Dylan. Please try." She could think of nothing else to say except, "I'll be waiting," and then she gently hung up the phone.

Chapter Three

He wasn't coming.

Absently Tess tapped the teaspoon against the palm of her hand. She glanced at the door of the small coffee shop for what surely must have been the millionth time.

Her eyes latched onto the large-faced clock behind the wide, white counter. Ten after nine. Nearly three hours had gone by since she'd called Dylan. Without thought, she raised her thumb to her mouth and searched nervously for a cuticle to worry.

He wasn't coming.

But he wouldn't *not* come. Would he? Not after the way she'd pleaded with him. Not when she'd just discovered—

"Here you go," the waitress said softly, setting a tall, icy glass of lemonade in front of Tess. "This is on the house. You won't sleep a wink tonight with all the coffee you've had."

A shadowy smile of appreciation barely curled the

corners of Tess's mouth. Sliding the empty coffee mug away from her several inches, she murmured, "Thank you," and reached for the glass.

"I wish you'd let me bring you something to eat," the waitress said.

The concern she heard in the woman's tone surprised Tess. She was a complete stranger to the waitress. Only in a town as small as Pine Meadow would total strangers take such an interest in another's welfare, she thought.

"Thanks," Tess said, noticing that the woman's name tag identified her as Sue. "But I couldn't eat a thing."

Sue's distress deepened into creases that marred her brow. "Are you sure you gave him the correct address? I mean, is there any chance he might have gone to some other coffee shop? There's a diner on High Street…"

This time Tess's surprise had her mouth inching open, her eyes blinking. She'd guessed Tess was waiting for someone. Waiting for a man.

Shifting her weight onto one hip, Sue absently slipped her pencil behind her ear, shook her head and said softly, "Honey, you're watching that door like you expect it to slip off its hinges and walk away. And no woman sits around for hours unless she's expecting a man. An *important* man."

The feathery-yet-intense inflection the waitress placed on the last short sentence clearly conveyed that she was sure that the man Tess awaited was no less than a lover. In any other circumstance, Tess was sure she'd have blushed. But the chaos reigning in her brain had her thoughts, her emotional responses, fragmented, splintered.

Dylan *was* an important man, she realized. Not because of any close relationship she shared with him, but because of *what* they had created. A precious child. A daughter. Erin.

The beautiful name whispered across her mind, and Tess latched onto it, focused on it and enjoyed a small moment of calm.

But the mere idea that her daughter was alive and well soon had her head churning all over again. However, she knew getting lost in the questions wouldn't help her one bit, so shoving the roiling thoughts aside, she looked up at the waitress.

"He *is* important," Tess admitted, although she didn't feel up to straightening out the woman's erroneous thinking by clarifying all that her statement meant.

"Well, you wait as long as you like," Sue told her. "We don't close till eleven."

The front door opened then, and Tess and the waitress were turning their heads to look before the small bells attached to the door's hinge barely had time to tinkle.

He looked good, Tess mused, her pulse pumping to life through veins that suddenly felt too small. Even though trouble clouded his eyes, the intense green of them had her breath catching in her throat. She remembered years ago how the long, wavy hair at the back of his neck would curl in silky tresses around her finger. But his chestnut hair was cut shorter now. In a more respectable fashion.

"Dylan! What brings you out at this time of night?" Sue greeted. "You're usually home with Erin, doing homework and housework, playing Daddy."

Tess didn't know why she was so taken aback that

the waitress knew Dylan—his shop was just up the block from the coffeehouse—but startled she was. However, maybe it wasn't so much that the waitress knew him, but the familiarity with which Sue greeted him that had Tess feeling so...odd.

Jealousy.

When she put a name to the emotion that was constricting her chest, she nearly gasped. Impossible! It was completely out of the question.

Then what was it?

Despite the anxiety shadowing his gaze, Dylan smiled at the waitress—and it was then that Tess correctly identified what she was feeling.

Envy. She was pea green with it. Before she could analyze the feeling further, though, Dylan's intense gaze was once again focused on her, silently demanding her attention.

"Let's go," he said, keeping the door propped open with one hand.

Tess felt as if she moved in slow motion as she made to rise. A small exhalation of shock erupted from the waitress. Looking up at the woman, Tess saw questions in Sue's eyes.

You've been waiting for *Dylan?* her gaze seemed to ask.

As if she were in a sleep-fogged dream, Tess decided she simply couldn't concern herself with the woman's curiosity. Tossing some bills on the table, she turned toward the door.

"I've got a fresh apple pie in the back," the waitress said to Dylan. "You sure I can't talk you into having a slice?"

"Some other time, Sue," Dylan said. "Erin's with a sitter, and she won't go to bed until I get home and put my foot down. Thanks anyway.'' Then his gaze darted to Tess and he curtly repeated, ''Let's go,'' his tone urging her to hurry.

The waitress softly called, ''Bye.''

And Tess was surprised to realize she was the one being spoken to. She nodded to the woman and offered her a distracted smile as she moved toward Dylan.

He was holding the door open and she was forced to brush the broad expanse of his chest with her shoulder as she passed between him and the doorjamb. The woodsy aroma of his cologne struck her full force and her instinct urged her to hesitate, to savor his heated scent. But luckily, he planted his hand firmly on the small of her back and propelled her out onto the sidewalk. Normally she'd have been incensed by such overbearing behavior, but she was relieved to follow his lead at the moment. How idiotic would she have looked if she'd paused to sniff the man's cologne?

The sight of him after so many years, the smell of him, the feel of his strong hand planted low on the small of her back, was all enough to send her senses into a tailspin.

Get a grip, girl!

''I don't need the whole town knowing my business,'' Dylan said, evidently in an effort to explain their rushed exit from the coffee shop.

''I understand,'' she automatically murmured, although she didn't really. Everyone in Pine Meadow already knew he had a daughter. People must realize the child had a mother. But she wasn't up to arguing. Not at the moment, anyway.

The whole world felt unbalanced. Off-kilter. But then, maybe it was just her. Of course, it was. Taking a deep inhalation of the cool night air, she tried to ground her thoughts, tried to stabilize her emotional equilibrium. But success was out of reach, she feared, because too much was happening too fast. She'd waited for him for hours. Hoped and prayed he'd come. Now that he had, she couldn't get a grasp on the situation. It was so unlike the normally cool, collected Dr. Tess Galloway.

"Like I told Sue," Dylan said, "Erin won't go to bed until I get home." He gave his wristwatch a darting glance in the dim light of the street lamp. "I can give you twenty minutes. Thirty, tops."

"I understand," she repeated.

"We can walk, or we can drive."

Again she parroted, "I understand."

His steps slowed. "Well—" then he stopped, lifting one hand palm up "—which will it be?"

The irritation she heard in his voice made her look into his face. There were lines bracketing his frowning mouth, and Tess had to fight the impulse to reach up and trace them with her fingertip. He looked so good. So ruggedly handsome. And that gorgeous green gaze, so full of—

"Tess!"

She jerked to attention. "I'm sorry, Dylan." Reaching up, she swiped her hand across her face. Her eyes raised to his and she repeated the apology a second time.

"You're acting like you're in a daze," he said. "What the hell is your problem?"

Anger reared its ugly head like a coiled and cornered snake, and it made her strike, viper-swift.

"How can you ask me that?" she said furiously, the dreamlike fog clouding her brain dissolving in an instant. "Do you have any idea what I'm going through here? Any idea what I'm dealing with?"

"Actually I don't," he said.

There was no trace of annoyance or anger in his quiet voice. If anything, he simply sounded weary.

"I have no idea what's happening with you," he continued. "No idea what brought you back to Pine Meadow. But I'm sure I'm about to find out."

What brought her back to Pine Meadow? She stopped on the sidewalk and turned to face him.

Her father's death—and the discovery of the mysterious bank account—was what had her returning to her hometown. Fuzzy thoughts hovered at the edge of her brain...fragments of ideas that needed connecting, but they flitted just out of reach. She dismissed them, intent on focusing on the situation at hand.

But it wasn't her father's death she'd been referring to when she'd asked Dylan if he understood what she was dealing with. She'd meant that she was facing the awesome realization that she had a child. A daughter. Erin.

Was Dylan purposefully missing the point just to shake her, make it utterly impossible to deal with him, with the situation she found herself in?

But, no, she thought, nearly shaking her head, he wasn't intentionally misconceiving anything. She remembered that he was under the impression that she'd abandoned Erin ten years ago. He didn't know that she had had no idea that her daughter was alive and living with her father in Pine Meadow.

"So what's it going to be?" he asked. "A walk? Or a drive?" He made no effort to hide his frustration.

Her heart rate accelerated. So did the thoughts, questions and doubts that bombarded her mind. Only moments ago in the coffee shop, Tess had felt a distinct delay of time, as though she were sleepwalking through a dream. But now the cadence of her existence seemed to speed up, his questions threatening to suck her into some churning chaos. Why would a simple decision throw her into such a panic? A walk or a drive. The choice wasn't life-altering.

"My car is right here." She pointed at the curb.

"Fine," he said. "A drive it is."

He approached the passenger door, opened it, and when she didn't move, he glanced at her. He tapped his wristwatch. "Thirty minutes, Tess," he reminded her.

His words, his body stance, his facial expression, even his deep green eyes, were all coated with a heavy layer of irritation that pulsed from him in palpable waves. The swells rippled, crested and crashed into her, driving her into motion.

"I understand," she said, digging into her purse for her keys as she rounded the rear of the car.

Thirty minutes! How could she ever ask him all the questions strafing her mind like a spray of bullets from an unrelenting machine gun? Did she focus only on Erin? Taking advantage of every second of the half hour allotted her to catch up on the last ten years of her daughter's life? Or should she start off by trying to convince Dylan that she hadn't known of Erin's existence?

"The car can't move until you put the key in the ignition and start the engine," he told her.

The impatient edge that clipped his words only caused her nerves to become even more frayed. "Of course," she said.

She jammed the key into the ignition and cranked

the engine to life. After slipping the car into gear, she
glanced over her shoulder and pulled onto the street—
and immediately realized that choosing to take a drive
had been a terrible mistake. How could she possibly
operate the car, deal with the stimulus of the passing
scenery, watch for pedestrians, traffic signs and stop-
lights *and* take part in a complicated, in-depth conversation with Dylan? The notion was ridiculous at
best, dangerous at worst.

Luckily she was traveling in the direction of Dylan's shop and she released an audible sigh of relief
when the building came into view.

"Would you mind," she said, braking at the stop
sign, "if I parked?"

He followed her gaze and evidently understood her
intent.

"Whatever," he said.

She pulled into the lot and shifted the gear stick
into Park, but before she cut the engine, she glanced
over at him.

The dashboard lights threw virescent light over his
face and hair, his chest, shoulders and arms. His eyes
were trained, unwavering, on his shop, his chin tipped
up, his jaw square and stubborn. Silence surrounded
him like a thick stone wall. He wasn't going to make
this easy, that was clear to her.

And then she detected the heady scent of his cologne floating on the still air inside the car. Her blood
pulsed faster. The temperature seemed to rise in the
close space, and she felt the impulse to lift the heavy
weight of her hair up off the back of her neck to cool
her skin, but she remained motionless.

Helplessly her gaze raked across his powerful chest,
and an unbidden image flashed before her eyes: her

young and trembling fingers splayed against his naked
pectorals, her heart pounding fearfully, excitingly, the
first time he'd tugged her on top of him during a passionate lovemaking episode.

She shook her head, banishing the erotic memory
from her mind.

So, she thought, her mind whirling, where was she
to start? She felt the seconds ticking by like a bomb
about to explode—a bomb that might not harm her,
but would surely whisk Dylan away and with him all
the important information about Erin for which she
was so desperate.

"Tell me about her."

Her whispered request sounded stentorian in the
tight, suddenly airless confines of the car.

He said nothing, and for a moment Tess feared he
meant to refuse to tell her anything. But then he spoke,
his gaze forward, his spine stiff.

"She's a great kid. She's healthy. Happy. She's…a
great kid."

Tess sat, breathless with anticipation as she waited
for him to continue.

But he didn't.

After a long moment, she said, "Is that all you're
going to say?"

Did she detect a shakiness in his long, controlled
sigh? But she didn't have time to reflect on the thought
before he turned his head to gaze at her.

"What do you want from me, Tess?" he asked.
"What is it you're looking for?"

"W-why," she stuttered, dumbfounded that he
could even ask those questions, "I want to know…
everything. I want to know what she looked like when
she was a baby. I want to know when she took her

first step. Smiled her first smile. What word she first spoke. I want to know when she lost her first tooth. When she stopped believing in Santa Claus. What her favorite—''

''Ahhh, I see now,'' he cut in, his tone filled to the brim with angry sarcasm. ''You want to be filled in on all those years you missed.''

''That's exactly what I want.''

Hostility strained and condensed the already cramped space in which they found themselves. His green eyes narrowed as he glared at her. Tess couldn't actually see it, she *felt* it.

''You don't deserve to be given any information,'' he said, his tone tight, barely controlled. ''You *chose* to separate yourself from Erin. You *chose* to send her back to Pine Meadow. You *chose* to have nothing whatsoever to do with—''

''I chose none of those things!'' she cried. She bit her bottom lip. This wasn't how she'd wanted to tell him. This wasn't how she'd meant for him to learn of her innocence. Smoothing her tongue across her lips, she inhaled, steeling herself to explain.

''I didn't know, Dylan,'' she told him. ''I didn't know my daughter was alive. Not until today. Not until—''

''You honestly don't expect me to believe that, do you?''

Even though she'd just moistened her lips, they felt as dry as road dust. ''I expect you to believe it,'' she said, ''because it's true.''

''Yeah, right,'' he murmured, turning his head to glance out the window. After a quick moment, he swiveled back to look at her through the gloom. His exhalation was short, audible and full of disgust.

''When I think about what you did, how you sent Erin packing, it makes me sick to my stomach.''

His words were like razor-edged knives hacking at her heart. But she wouldn't allow him to wound her with his opinion of her. Not again. He'd done it before. Ten years ago when she was just a tender, innocent teen. She refused to let him hurt her again with his asinine assumptions.

''If you insist on believing that I would do such a thing—'' She halted, the unspeakable words lumping in her throat. A small cough cleared a pathway so she could proceed. ''That I could knowingly, and willingly, give up a precious child, then by all means, go on believing it. It's no skin off my nose.''

''None of this has been any skin off your nose, has it?''

She hated the fact that his sarcasm stung her so. ''How can you say that? Think of everything I've missed!''

''All I can think of—''

His quiet tone was irritatingly unflappable.

''—is all that you've *gained*.''

''All I've…'' The two small words were all she was able to utter before her bewilderment over the hidden meaning of his statement had her frowning in silence. What on earth could he possibly mean?

The night seemed to grow bleaker, more shadowed. But she was still able to see him reach out in the darkness. His touch could almost have been described as a caress as his fingertips trailed a slow moving path along the dashboard's rounded edge. She remembered vividly what it was like being on the receiving end of his gentle touch. Her heart tripped in her chest, heat flickering to life deep in the very center of her being. Stop!

"Nice wheels," he commented. "Still has that new car smell."

Tess tensed. What was he getting at? she wondered warily.

"Smells of something else, too," he continued. "Money."

Something inside her shriveled at the acerbity evinced in his tone. Why shouldn't she have a nice car? She'd worked long and hard. For years. Gone without for the sole purpose of her education. The automobile hadn't been that pricey. And it wasn't as if she'd paid cash. She was making payments. Just like everyone else in the nation. Credit, the good ol' American standby. Another point in her favor, she thought, was that she hadn't made the purchase until she'd procured the job with the family medical practice.

"Too much money," he went on, "for the salary of say, a waitress like Sue, or a grocery clerk, or a shoe salesperson."

Blinking in the darkness, Tess knew he was just gearing up for an attack, but she still didn't quite see where he was heading with his argument.

Then he turned to face her. "Professionally manicured nails. That silk getup. Leather pumps." He added as an aside, "Italian imports, from the look of them." Hesitating only a moment, he asked, "Tell me, Tess, what do you do for a living?"

Even though she hadn't a clue why she should feel ashamed, her face flamed at the mysterious connotation concealed in what he said. She did her own nails, thank you very much! And she'd never in a million years admit to him that *he* had been her reasoning behind splurging on the new dress and shoes. The mere idea that she might meet Dylan in Pine Meadow had her spending two careful hours selecting this dress, these shoes. But now she fervently wished she'd worn nothing more than her faded jeans, an old sweater and her ratty sneakers.

He didn't give her time to answer his questions before he suggested, "Corporate executive? Stock investor? Lawyer?" His tone deepened as he said, "Whatever you do, it takes an education. And knowing your father and his unwavering plans for your schooling, you've done nothing but focus on yourself. Your education and your career. So what you've gained, I'd say, is ten years free from the hassles and responsibilities of child rearing so you could set yourself up."

She actually gasped softly when he'd finally revealed his bitter gripe against her. Even though she'd promised herself she wouldn't allow him to hurt her, tears stung her eyes, blurred her vision. She'd be damned if she let him see her cry.

"Set myself up? You're crazy." She was pleased that the pain and insult caused by his accusations wasn't evident in her voice.

"So answer my question," he quietly taunted. "What do you do for a living that allows you to afford this beautiful car and the expensive clothes?"

Earning her medical degree had made her feel more proud than any other accomplishment. But now Dylan succeeded in making her feel lousy about it. He made it seem as though she'd tossed aside her child to get where she was. That simply wasn't true. But Dylan wasn't going to believe that.

Finally she forced herself to admit, "I'm a doctor. A medical doctor."

"Ah…"

Tess detested the haughtiness he expressed.

"…four years of college, four years of med school," he said. "Couple years of residency and you're set for life. That's about how it works, isn't it?"

Tess was confident she could hide her hurt feelings, but letting his blatant censure go without an argument was beyond her.

"I would never, *ever* have put myself before my daughter," she said, her throat feeling raw and painful. "If I had known—"

"Come off it, Tess," he cut in. "Don't sit there and lie. You knew."

"I'm not lying," she insisted.

"How can a woman give birth and not realize whether or not her child lived?"

The blood in her veins seemed to slow as guilt froze it into icy slush. She whispered, "Don't you think I've been asking myself that same question all afternoon? All evening? Ever since I saw that little girl's face, I've been…" She swallowed hard, let the rest of her thought fade as she bit down on her bottom lip and turned to look out into the night. In an instant, she was thrown back into the past.

Heavy sheets of rain had been falling the night she'd gone into labor. Fear was what she remembered most. Fear. And soul-splitting pain. Oh, her father had tried to comfort her. The nurse and doctor, too. But the pain had been so intense it seemed to be never ending. The hours had ticked by at an agonizingly slow rate. She'd crooned over and over for the baby to come. Her cherished baby.

Through the months of her pregnancy, she'd wished and prayed for a baby boy. A baby boy who looked just like Dylan. She knew her father would have had a fit if he'd known how she dreamed of her son's dark brown hair, his sea-green eyes and a face that would remind her every single day of the man she desperately loved.

Yes, Dylan had wounded her terribly with his hateful words, with his vicious rejection, but that didn't stop her from loving him. From wanting him. Since he refused to be with her, she'd spend her life caring and rearing the child they had created together. The child conceived through their love.

Her labor pains worsened, and the doctor grew worried and edgy. His anxious expression, his nervous demeanor, had frightened her more than the pain ever had. At last the doctor decided to take the baby through cesarean section rather than allowing her to give birth naturally. The last thing Tess remembered was calling out for her father and then pleading with the doctor to tell her what was going on, what was wrong with her baby. But her sweaty cries, her frantic questions, had gone unanswered as a nurse plunged a needle into Tess's vein and she'd slipped into a deep, unnatural sleep.

When she'd awakened, her father had been right there by her side, holding her hand. Oh, how she'd cried when he'd told her that her baby had been stillborn. But her grief had been relatively silent, hot, scalding tears had burned their way down her face, as her father had patted her hand and whispered consolingly, "This is all for the best. It's all for the best."

She'd only seen the doctor one other time when he'd come to check her sutures and release her from the hospital. He hadn't been able to look her in the eye. Tess had always thought that was because he'd felt badly that her baby had died. But now she knew better. Now she knew he'd been too ashamed to lift his gaze to hers, too embarrassed by the fact that he'd somehow stolen her baby from her.

Anger smoldered inside her chest. Anger at the years of grief she'd needlessly suffered. At her father for not protecting her. At the doctor for sneaking and conniving. At all the years she'd lost with her little girl. At Dylan for not believing her when she told him the truth.

"You can't argue with the cold, hard facts," Dylan said, drawing her from the past. "You left Pine Meadow and seven and a half months later you sent Erin back." He sighed. "I'm not saying it was all your fault. You were young. I'm sure your father talked you into—"

"Don't you speak ill of my father." The poisonous venom she heard in her own words startled her.

"But he was so adamantly against—"

"He's dead," she told him bluntly. "My father is dead."

A moment of silence followed the bombshell she dropped.

Dylan smoothed his fingers over his chin in evident contemplation. Finally he said, "I'm sorry. I'm truly sorry for you." His tone softened. "Ever since you left the shop this afternoon, I've been racking my brain trying to figure out why you came back. Why did she wait ten years? I kept asking myself. Well—" he paused, looking at her across the darkness "—now I know."

There they were again, Tess noticed. Those fuzzy, disconnected thoughts fluttering, butterflylike, at the outer edges of her brain. Ideas that needed piecing together like a jigsaw puzzle. Notions that had to do with her father and the reason she'd returned to Pine Meadow.

"Your dad's death," he began slowly and then faltered. "His dying has made you want to make things right, is that it?"

It hadn't been her father's death that had brought her back to Pine Meadow. *It had been the bank account!* The huge amount of money sitting in Minster Banking and Trust.

All the pieces were there, floating before her closed eyelids. Her father. Her daughter. Her lover. A large sum of money. Ten missing years. Blood whooshed through her ears as her panicked heart accelerated to a frantic beat.

It had been quite natural to make the doctor who had delivered her baby the conniving, evil culprit. She'd never have suspected her father would have been a party to anything so horrible, so sinister. Her father had loved her. Hadn't he?

The pieces of this awful puzzle hovered and spun, just waiting to be snapped together.

Her eyes went wide as she looked at Dylan. Had he been part of the plot to steal away her child? she wondered. Had the whole world been against her all those years ago?

Feeling her hands begin to shake violently, she grasped the steering wheel to steady them, but not before Dylan's frown alerted her that he'd noticed how she trembled.

He was waiting for her to answer his question, but for the life of her, she couldn't remember what that question was.

She needed time. She needed space. She needed to think. Clearly. She needed to figure out this mess. She desperately needed to get away from Dylan. Now.

"You have to go," she blurted, barely holding herself together. "Your car is just up the block. A two minute walk. You should go."

"But—"

"Erin's waiting," she reminded him. Her composure was slipping, slipping. "Surely our thirty minutes are up. We'll talk some more. Tomorrow. I'll come to your shop. While Erin's at school."

He'd evidently become so wrapped up in their conversation that he'd forgotten all about the time. Darting a glance at his watch, he said, "Well, I really should—"

"Go," she told him, her tone firmer, louder than she'd intended.

After a short, bewildered nod of farewell, Dylan got out of the car and walked away. Tess watched him in the rearview mirror until his form became obscured by the darkness.

Finally she could hold on no further. "Oh, Daddy, how could you?" she whispered. Then she buried her face in her hands and wept.

Chapter Four

Her father had sold her baby.

Tess sat in the car for an eternity feeling stunned and empty. She sat there until the air grew stuffy and stale. She sat there until there were no more tears in her to shed.

How could something so horrific happen to her? she wondered.

Her father had sold her baby.

The idea had floated in and out of her brain dozens of times yet she still couldn't quite seem to grasp it. The concept was simply too huge, too awful. She couldn't get her hands, or her mind, around it.

Her father had loved her. Had sacrificed so much for her. Cared for her. Nurtured her. To think that he'd purposefully taken away what would have been the most precious thing in her life—*and he'd profited from the act.* It was simply unfathomable.

When she'd found the bank account and all those unopened statements, she hadn't known what to think.

The notion that her father had accepted money from Dylan's parents for taking her out of town, out of their son's life, had been the most logical conclusion. But now…after seeing Erin with her own eyes, realizing that her child hadn't been stillborn, but stolen…

No, she told herself firmly, finally finding the guts to admit the truth. Not stolen. *Sold.* By her father. Her own flesh and blood. There could be no other explanation for that large sum of money sitting in Minster Savings and Loan under an account listing her father as owner.

But who had supplied the money? Dylan's parents? His tyrannical father, his overbearing mother? Or had Dylan been the buying partner in the torrid baby-selling bargain?

He was Erin's father. He had the most to gain by offering Tess's dad a deal. Maybe Dylan had decided he hadn't wanted to live his life with the daughter of a shoe repairman, a girl from the wrong side of town, a girl with no gentility climbing around in her family tree, a girl with no prospects, no future. Maybe he had decided he hadn't wanted his child's mother, but he *had* wanted his child. That would make perfect sense.

But wait! her subconscience silently nudged her. Why would Dylan make such an angry fuss, insisting that she knew all about Erin? That she'd sent the child back to Pine Meadow without a second thought?

A smoke screen, pure and simple. He wanted to cover his horrible deed. And making her feel guilty, making her out to be the bad guy, was the perfect way to do it.

But Dylan Minster wasn't that kind of person. The statement whispered across her mind.

Tess heaved a sigh, reminding herself that ten years

had passed. Anything could happen to a person over that amount of time. Besides, hadn't he changed even *before* she'd left Pine Meadow? Hadn't he rejected her with mean and hateful words that she wouldn't have believed could have come from him unless she'd actually heard them with her own ears?

She didn't know Dylan. Didn't know who he was. Or who he'd become.

Tread carefully. The susurrus warning echoed in her brain. *You don't know if he's guilty. You don't know for sure.*

No, she didn't, she admitted silently. But she meant to find out. And if she discovered he was behind this terrible, twisted mess, then she'd show him as much mercy as he'd shown her all those years ago.

None.

"Ya know, Dad," Erin said, her voice small, "I'm feeling kinda queasy in my stomach."

Dylan frowned and studied his daughter's face for signs of illness, flushed cheeks or a bleary-looking gaze. Maybe the headache Erin suffered yesterday was a prerequisite of the flu or something. Funny how she hadn't mentioned feeling ill until now.

Their before-school ritual was already well underway. Erin had eaten her breakfast, she'd picked out her clothes and changed into them, she'd made her bed. If she wasn't feeling well she usually announced that fact well before now, so Dylan was surprised to hear her complain. But then, he thought, maybe he shouldn't have been. He had an idea what this queasy stomach was all about.

"You really should go to school today," he said, keeping any hint of censure out of his tone. His daughter had been hit with quite a surprise yesterday; what she needed was understanding, not an overbearing father breathing down her neck. "Thanks to your grandmother, you're all caught up, but if you miss another day of school..."

"Yeah—" Erin rolled her eyes dramatically "—thanks to Grandmother I had two full pages of math problems to do and a chapter of social studies to review last night. I missed my favorite TV show and—"

"All right, now," he gently admonished. "Grandma only did what she thought was best for you."

The child giggled delightedly. "If she ever heard you call her *Grandma* she'd twist your ears into pretzels."

Dylan grinned at his daughter's reflection in the mirror. "She probably would. So that's our little secret, agreed?" He reached out his index finger.

Automatically, Erin curled hers around her father's and gave one quick, gentle tug. This had been their secret "handshake" for as long as Dylan could remember. He picked up the hairbrush.

"So, what's it going to be today?" he asked, drawing the brush through her long red hair. "Leave it loose? Ponytail? Braids?"

"A braid, please," she told him. "Just one. Straight down the back."

"One braid, coming up." He parted Erin's hair into three neat sections and began to plait, strand over strand. His fingers were deft and he executed the task with the ease of someone who had performed it time and again. He had. For as long as Erin's hair had been long enough to braid. Oh, he hadn't always been as skilled as he was now. Erin had worn more than one lopsided braid. But plaiting hair was like playing a musical instrument, cooking a perfect meat loaf or tuning a car's engine—practice made perfect.

He enjoyed this early-morning ritual with Erin. Fixing her breakfast and then cleaning up the dishes while she got herself dressed. He always brushed her hair, otherwise she would walk out the door with her bangs sticking straight up. He'd pack her lunch while she packed her book bag and then she'd kiss him goodbye before running for the big yellow school bus that stopped for her up the block.

Yes, he relished his mornings with Erin, he thought, reaching for a fabric-covered elastic band he used to secure the braid. These mornings helped him start his day with a smile. Even on days when he didn't feel like smiling. Days just like today.

He hadn't meant to hurt Tess's feelings last night when they had talked. All he'd been looking for was a little honesty. Did she really expect him to believe she had no idea Erin was living in Pine Meadow? That simply wasn't possible—

"Maybe," Erin began haltingly, staring wide-eyed at him in the mirror, "I ought to go to the shop with you today."

Here it comes, Dylan mused. That expression on her darling little face, that breathy suggestion, both were packed to the hilt with turmoil. This had nothing to do with an upset stomach. This had to do with Tess. He'd have felt safe betting his last dollar on it.

"I think you need to go to school," he remarked, knowing full well an argument was brewing.

"B-but *what if she comes?*"

Awe, fear and excitement churned in that small

whispered question. Dylan realized it was only natural for Erin to want to see her mother. He only wished he knew what was in Tess's head. What did the woman hope her visit to Pine Meadow would accomplish? He wouldn't allow Tess to hurt Erin. That, he simply wouldn't tolerate.

"She probably will come to the shop today," he told Erin.

The glow of expectation in her chocolate-brown gaze twisted his heart.

"But you, young lady," he said, "will be in school. Tess, er, ah," he stammered, then corrected, "your mother and I have some talking to do—"

"I want to see her."

Dylan kept his voice calm, but insistent. "I know you do. And there will be plenty of time for that. *After* school."

"Ya mean it?" She actually squirmed with the anticipation. "Today?"

"Hold still," he said, hating the all-too-human feelings of possessiveness that reared up inside him. But he muscled them to the back of his brain, logically understanding that meeting Tess could very well be a wonderful event in his daughter's life. He brushed the tiny tail of the braid around his finger until it curled prettily and then patted her shoulder. "All done. Time to pack up your books. The bus will be by soon."

She hurried off toward the kitchen, as if rushing the day to begin would somehow make this afternoon arrive sooner. Anxiety knotted in his stomach as he weighed the possibilities of Erin meeting her mother. Good experience, or bad, he knew everything hinged on Tess. He had no control over the woman and that worried him.

Dylan was wrapping a cheese sandwich in plastic wrap when Erin asked, "You don't think she'll leave town without talking to me at least once, do you?"

He didn't like the anxiety he saw marring her young brow. "Du-uh," he said, hoping his dopey tone would bring a smile to her face, "now why would she do a dumb thing like that?"

But Erin's mouth remained a taut line as she shrugged. Then she said firmly, "You get her to stay at least until I get home from school."

A chuckle eased from his throat. "Honey, I don't expect I could get Tess Galloway to do anything that she didn't want to do."

He remembered a time that wasn't so. A time when Tess would have done anything, gone anywhere, to please him. Hell, she'd have walked through fire if he'd given her the least indication that that's what would have made him happy. But that had been years ago. A whole other lifetime, really.

After a quick kiss on the cheek, Erin went running out the door, and Dylan was left alone in a houseful of troubled thoughts.

Tess Galloway. My, how that woman had changed his life. Well, she hadn't been quite a woman back then. Spindly teen would have been a more apt description, all elbows and knees, when he'd first met her. But then all those years ago he couldn't have been defined as anything other than lean and lanky, himself.

Reaching for his mug, Dylan took a sip of steamy coffee, and smiled as he swallowed. He could picture the first time he'd seen her as if it were happening right this moment rather than years and years ago. He'd walked into her father's shoe repair shop looking for someone to put some new holes into his favorite black leather belt. His mother had given him such grief that morning, telling him to throw away the worn belt and buy a new one. But Dylan had been stubborn. He didn't want a new one. He saw his parents as extravagant and excessive when it came to buying new things, tossing their money around. So what if he'd lost a few pounds? Growth spurts did that to a guy every now and then. All he needed were a couple of new holes in the belt and it would serve him just fine.

As he thought back on it now, Dylan figured it was his desire to rebel against his mother and father about the stupid belt more than anything else that took him into Harry Galloway's shop. And the fact that the shop was located in the Bowers made it all the more perfect. Him patronizing a business located in the wrong side of town would really tick off his parents but good.

The door of the shop stuck when he tried to open it, and he'd had to give it a good push. The air was dry and hot inside, the strong smell of leather and shoe polish hitting him like a solid wall. The girl behind the counter was young, the sun shining through the big front windows gleaming like molten fire against her long, wavy red hair. She smiled a hello, and unwittingly Dylan's posture straightened, his shoulders squared.

Immediately he'd been taken aback by his reaction. Why on earth would he feel the need to strut his stuff for this young colt-of-a-girl? She was too young for his interest. Much too young. Why, she couldn't be more than thirteen or fourteen. In the mind of a seventeen-year-old, a *high school senior* for goodness' sake, this girl was just a kid, and being attracted to a kid was worse than catching a case of the plague.

But as he explained to her what he needed, and she

took the belt from his hands, his gaze was drawn again and again to those twinkling, nut-brown eyes of hers, all that creamy skin speckled with tiny freckles across her nose and forehead. She was cute. There was no way around it.

They became friends from the very first. Secret friends. If Dylan's buddies ever discovered that he spent many of his afternoons with a kid, they'd have laughed him into tomorrow. Many times he told himself he should stay away from her. But his motorcycle seemed to steer itself into the Bowers, seemed to park itself under the shady trees of the tiny little scrap of land the Pine Meadow planning board tried to pass off as a formal walking garden in the town's only park.

Tess Galloway was fourteen, she haughtily assured him. The proud manner in which her chin tipped up made him laugh, and she became angry. But it didn't take much from him to make her smile again, though.

She was so easy to talk to, and she seemed to understand him. And his problems. Mainly his contempt for his parents. She didn't share it, didn't pass judgment. She simply understood. Dylan could never have complained to his other friends. How could he? From their point of view, he was a young man who was practically offered the world on a silver tray. Who was he to bemoan the expensive clothes he wore, the motorcycle he drove, the boarding school he attended? But Tess quietly listened and never criticized. She cared about him. At a time when he felt that no one else really and truly did. He liked that about her. He liked it a lot. And he guessed that was what kept him coming back to visit her in that pathetic little garden.

They were friends. Nothing more. And it was a relationship that they'd had to hide. From her father.

From his parents. From his school buddies. But the times he spent with her were some of the most memorable of his life. He felt he could have told her anything. Everything. And he did.

For nearly eighteen months they met in secret. They talked and laughed and philosophized. They shared their experiences. They cried together. They learned from each other, and grew. They knew everything there was to know about each other.

If he were to be completely honest, he'd have to admit that he had known Tess adored him. Almost from the very start. He saw it in the doe-eyed expressions she graced him with, in the way she hung on his every word. Yeah, he'd been aware that she loved him. That she wanted more from their relationship. From him. But he forced himself to keep their alliance a "friends only" kind of thing. Completely platonic. She was too important to him to mess up what they had with too much emotion. Besides, she was too young to take things to a higher level...a physical level. He promised himself he wouldn't allow it.

But each passing month made keeping his promise more and more difficult. He longed to caress her delicate, pale cheek, to kiss her soft, full lips. Still, he held tight to his silent pledge even though he knew Tess would have eagerly given herself to him.

Then on Tess's sixteenth birthday, Dylan could stand it no longer and he offered to take her for a ride on his motorcycle. They had driven out to the dense woods on the outskirts of Pine Meadow. That had been the day that had changed their relationship. Forever.

Dylan sighed, and like the dust-kicking wheels of a hopped-up sports car, his memories spun away out of sight.

The teenage Tess had been gangly and thin, he remembered, she'd been awkward in her still-developing body, but she'd been the most caring and compassionate person he'd ever met. And she'd stolen his heart.

He couldn't help but notice how the years had changed her. The woman who had stood in his parking lot yesterday afternoon, silky fabric softly draping luscious curves, short hemline revealing a mile of shapely legs, had been no less than utterly gorgeous. She was enough to cause a man to suffer restless insomnia, and he knew damned well she was behind all his tossing and turning last night. Even now, as he imagined her lush body, her softly curling red hair, her wine-colored lips, those deep mahogany eyes, that pert, little nose, he felt a wrenching, a tightening, down low in his gut.

Stop! What the devil was the matter with him?

His chance with Tess was over. Long over. Any opportunity the two of them might have had together had been murdered—killed by mistakes both of them had made in the past.

Lust. That was it, he realized. Pure male lust.

So he had a yearning. So what? He could handle it. Certainly she wouldn't be in town for that long. A few days. A week at the most. He could control his physical desires.

He took a sip of his stone-cold coffee and grimaced. The clock on the wall made him curse under his breath, and he dropped the mug into the sink. Seven forty-five! And he wasn't even dressed yet. He rushed toward his bedroom, knowing full well that, for the first time in his life, he'd be opening the shop late. All because he'd sat dawdling over his memories of Tess Galloway.

* * *

"Well, ma'am," the young, suit-clad bank officer said. He'd introduced himself as Pete, Pete Taylor. "I really don't have any other information on the account. Other than what I've already given you, that is."

Tess sat back in the cushioned seat, depression quickly seeping into every pore. For some stupid reason she'd thought this morning's trip to Minster Savings and Loan would answer all her questions. Or at least some of them. As it turned out, she was just as much in the dark about the money as she'd been when she'd walked through those thick, double-wide glass doors fifteen minutes ago.

"That's too bad," she told the man. "I'd hoped to find out where the money came from. You see, with my father's death last month—"

"I'd like to tell you again how sorry I am to hear that," Mr. Pete Taylor remarked automatically.

Tess murmured appreciation. "I came upon the bankbook while going through his things. My father never said a word to me about this account."

The young man's brows raised in surprise. "It is odd that he didn't speak of this to you, especially since you're listed here as his beneficiary." He peered at the computer screen closer. "Another odd thing...the account shows no activity." He looked back at her. "I don't mean little activity. I mean none. Other than the accruing interest, there have been no deposits, no withdrawals." His mouth curled into a soft smile. "But this is really wonderful for you. A nice, tidy hidden treasure you've unearthed."

He might think so, but Tess certainly didn't. This money was more like a heavy boulder tied around her neck, a weight that seemed to grow heavier with each passing moment. For that reason, she didn't respond, but sat there, motionless.

Evidently becoming uncomfortable with the silence that had settled over them, the man cleared his throat, his smile fading, and he glanced back at his computer terminal.

"You know," he said, "this account is over ten years old. I've only been with the bank for two years. I could call upstairs..."

Tess felt the hairs on the back of her neck prickle. *Upstairs* was sure to mean the executive offices of the bank.

"...I could talk to Mrs. Minster—she's the president of the bank—maybe she'll know something about your father's account."

"No." The word erupted from her lips so suddenly that the bank officer started. "No, thank you, Mr. Taylor," she said, this time with a little more decorum.

The very last thing in the world she needed right now was to have Helen Minster alerted to her presence in her bank. In her town. Oh, Tess hadn't fooled herself into thinking she could stay in Pine Meadow without the town's matriarch discovering her presence. She knew Dylan's mother would find out, sooner or later. Tess just opted for later, is all.

Then she asked. "*Mrs.* Minster is the bank's president? When I lived in Pine Meadow, Mr. Minster was in charge."

Pete Taylor nodded. "He died a while back. It's been years now."

"Oh." So Dylan's father had passed away, too.

"Well..." Pete paused as if he was at a loss as to what to do next. Then his expression became once again animated as an idea evidently came to him.

"How about if I start the paperwork to have the account turned over to you?" he said. "You did bring a death certificate with you?" He looked at her expectantly.

"Yes, I did," she told him. "But..." Tess didn't understand why she hesitated, but something inside her vied for her attention, like two feet planted firmly on a car's brake pedal. "I'm not sure I want to do that just yet."

He seemed bewildered by her hesitance. His suggestion made sense, she realized. It was only logical for the account to be put into her name. But for some reason—

That money was tainted! The words came into her mind, loud and clear. That money was defiled. She didn't want to have anything to do with it.

She stood suddenly. "I'll be in town a while. I'll come back." Then she turned toward the door.

"Wait," he called.

The doorknob was still in her hand as she twisted to face him.

"At least take the paperwork with you." He reached into his drawer and pulled out a form. "Bring this in with the appropriate information filled in. And I'll need a copy of the death certificate." Then he further offered, "I have access to a copy machine, if that will help..."

He was so eager to please, she realized. She went to his desk, smiled and took the paper from him. "I do want to thank you. You've been most helpful."

"It's been my pleasure."

Back out in the bank's main lobby, Tess took a moment to exhale a disappointed sigh. This visit had been pretty close to useless.

The large, wide-open space of the bank lobby was built in an atrium fashion. One side of the room was lined with a high counter behind which smartly dressed tellers made transactions for Pine Meadow residents and businesspeople. Several free-standing cubicles were arranged in the center of the room. An elegant staircase led to the second floor where office doors lined the wall directly above the teller counter. Tess couldn't seem to tear her eyes from the office doors lining the upper landing.

That, she knew, was the "upstairs" to which the bank officer had just referred. Those were the executive offices. A shiver coursed across her skin.

That woman.

Tess couldn't see Helen Minster sitting at a desk behind one of those heavy wooden doors, but that didn't matter. She could picture Dylan's mother, just the same.

Thoughts of that woman conjured feelings in Tess that threatened to overwhelm her. The stern, disapproving Helen Minster had thought Tess worthless. *Less* than worthless. Tess, Helen Minster had thought, was a girl from the wrong side of town looking to get ahead by clinging to her son, and that was something that she simply wouldn't allow to happen. In the matriarch's eyes, the penniless daughter of a shoe repairman was not good enough for Dylan. And because Helen Minster had thought it, voiced it, Tess had believed it. For a long, long time.

One of the office doors on the second floor opened, and a middle-aged woman stepped out onto the landing. Tess recognized Dylan's older sister. The woman knocked on the door of the adjacent office. The door opened, and Helen Minster came into Tess's view.

Unwittingly she dipped her head, averting her face from view. She should leave the bank. Now. She should move one foot in front of the other, until she was standing out on the sidewalk. But paralysis seemed to have frozen her legs.

All she could think about was the huge sum of money that had been sitting in Helen Minster's bank for years. Tess thought of what that money had bought. What that money had cost her. Helplessly Tess glanced upward.

As though the elderly woman had some sixth sense and realized she was being watched, she paused in her conversation and glanced down at the lobby below. Her gaze scanned the sparse, quiet group of employees and patrons, and came to rest on Tess.

Immediately Tess cast her eyes to the floor, turning her face away.

Worthless. The word rang through her head. Less than worthless.

The blast of anger that exploded inside her rocked her from the top of her head to the very soles of her feet. How dare that woman make her feel inferior?

Yes, she might have been born and raised in the wrong part of town. But that happened to lots of good-hearted, reputable people. And yes, she might be the daughter of a shoe repairman. But her father...

The thought faltered when her father—or rather, her father's behavior came to mind. Her father hadn't been honest. Hadn't been good-hearted. Hadn't been reputable. She'd just realized that last night. Tess felt her chin tremble.

Lord, she had to get out of this building!

But she stood firm as she felt something odd stir inside her. Whatever it was grew and stretched.

Determination. That's what it was.

She hadn't done anything wrong. She was a blameless victim in this mess. Besides that, she wasn't a mousy, easily frightened teenager any longer. She was a grown woman. An educated woman. A woman filled with a sturdy resolve to solve a horrible mystery—a mystery in which Dylan's mother was most probably somehow embroiled.

Her shoulders squared, her spine straightened, and Tess lifted her chin slowly, raised her gaze until she was looking directly, steadily into Helen Minster's eyes.

I'm here! she wanted to shout. I'm back in town. And I'm not leaving without telling my daughter the truth!

But she wouldn't make a scene. It just wasn't in her. So, she simply stood there, letting the elderly woman get a good, long look at her. Only then did she walk out the door into the bright morning sunshine.

Chapter Five

Rounding the corner of the one-story brick building, she caught sight of him working under a shade tree and she stopped, deciding on a whim to give herself a moment to take stock of the situation; what she should say, how she should act.

She grimaced, her shoulders inching toward her ears. Who was she kidding? Tess mused, having enough sense to feel irritated by the blatant lie. Her objective in pausing wasn't to plan out a strategy—it was to stare at him, plain and simple.

He was poised over the open hood of a car, tinkering with the engine. The fabric of his cotton shirt was smooth across the broad expanse of his shoulders, his faded denim jeans defined hard thighs and a tight butt. She could no more stop the appreciative grin that tugged at the corners of her mouth than she could have stopped time itself.

You're not here for this, her logical mind chided from what seemed a far distance.

Oh, why don't you just shut up and enjoy the view?
a fun-loving voice responded.

Clapping her fingers over her lips, she stifled the
delighted chuckle that bubbled up into her throat. She
hadn't heard a peep from the gleeful side of herself
in...ages. She'd been too focused on learning the anatomy of the human body and how it worked with the
chemistry of modern medicine.

She'd only relished the sight of Dylan's denim-clad
rear for a few seconds when she watched his hand
snake out toward the toolbox that was too far away
from him. She knew that, any moment, he would have
to lift up his head to locate the toolbox, and she was
mortified to think she might get caught standing here
gawking at him.

''Hello,'' she called, just as he straightened his
back.

Fall had the air feeling clean and cool, but the leaves
on the trees were still a vibrant green. Sunlight filtered
through them now, burnishing Dylan's brown hair
with a rich chestnut hue. A strange thrill shot through
her when he turned toward her, his emerald eyes settling on her face. However, just as she'd suppressed
the laughter that had threatened to surface, she did the
same to this giddy swell that rolled over her like an
ocean wave. These emotions had no place here. No
place at all.

''Tess.''

Not even a hint of a smile softened the straight line
of his mouth—the same mouth that, years ago, had
been so gentle, so coaxing against hers, the same
mouth that... Her hands balled into fists at her side.
Her vivid sensuous memories of Dylan were hamper-
ing her battle against the strong physical attraction she

felt for him—the attraction she'd already decided she couldn't allow herself to feel.

When she realized that her name was all she was going to receive from him by way of a greeting, her shoulders sagged with a sigh.

"What can I say to convince you?" she asked quietly, struggling to focus on the problems of the here and now.

His brows raised. "Convince me?"

"Yes," she said. "What will make you believe I'm not a horrible person? That I'm innocent of wrongdoing?"

Dylan was quiet for some moments. He centered his attention on the tools in the metal box. He reached in and picked up a ratchet of some kind and then set it back down in its allotted space. She remained silent, unmoving, determined to wait him out for an answer.

Finally he lifted his eyes to hers. "I don't know, Tess," he told her. "I'm not sure there's anything you can say that would convince me."

Her heart grew heavy, but she didn't speak.

"But I've been thinking about our conversation last night," he went on. "About our...disagreement. And I think it would be best if we just let it go for now. This shouldn't be about you and me. This shouldn't be about what did or didn't happen in the past. This is about Erin. Period."

She studied his face. What he said made sense. Sounded mature. Wise. Now all she had to do was figure out if he was being honest and up-front with her, or if this was just more smoke he was blowing to cover up the truth about how their daughter came to be in Pine Meadow.

Whether this idea was more deception on Dylan's

part, or pure concern, it really didn't matter. Because what he said was the truth. Erin was all that mattered to her. The rest could wait. She had plenty of time to discover the facts about the past.

"You're right," Tess said. "This is about Erin. Period."

Her statement might have been described as a little misleading, but she didn't feel badly about that. She had a right to know the full, unadulterated truth. And she had every intention of exerting that right. But she'd bide her time. For now, she was content to focus on Erin.

"So," she began softly. "Did you tell her? About who I am, I mean?"

Dylan's gaze didn't waver. "I told her."

"How did she react?"

Some fleeting, unreadable emotion passed over his face. Was that concern? A scowl of anger? A frown of worry? However, her building anxiety and excitement regarding her daughter didn't allow her to ponder Dylan's emotional state for long.

"Well," she prompted him, suddenly feeling as eager as a newborn pup, "w-what did she have to say?"

His shoulder hitched up the merest fraction of an inch. "Erin's an intelligent child. She's curious by nature."

The stoicism evinced in his tone didn't disguise his defensiveness. Her whole body relaxed, her heart softening, when she realized he felt threatened by her presence.

"I have no intention of coming between you and Erin," she told him.

"That will never happen."

There was a clear challenge in his voice, in the rigid

set of his shoulders, his narrowed gaze. She couldn't help the contradiction he made in suggesting they avoid arguments by letting go of their differences, and now here he was egging for a fight.

As far as she could see, there were two avenues open to her; she could accept and become embroiled in the controversy he was offering, or continue to try to assuage his fear—the fear that was the underlying cause of his harsh tone and the opposition in his green eyes. Because she could easily imagine what he must be feeling, and because she did like his idea of focusing on Erin, Tess decided to continue along the pacifying route.

She offered him a small smile and softly said, "Then we agree." Her smile widened. "That's good, don't you think?"

It was immediately obvious that he sensed the olive branch she was offering. He averted his eyes, almost shamefully, and when he looked up at her again, he slowly nodded his agreement.

"Erin can't wait to meet you," he admitted quietly. He shook his head, chuckling softly to himself. "So much so," he went on, "that she tried to get me to let her stay home from school today."

A rush of pure joy rolled over her. "She did?"

"Mm-hmm." He nodded again. "She complained of an upset stomach. But I knew she was just excited and nervous about meeting you. I told her she had to go to school, and that the two of you could talk this afternoon. After school was over."

Her daughter had wanted to skip school in order to meet her! The idea made her giddy with pleasure.

"I know what she means about having an upset stomach." Tess absently flattened her palm against her midriff. "I've had anxious butterflies flapping inside me, too. But I am glad you made her go to school. I wouldn't like to be the cause of her missing a day." After a moment, she asked, "Does she like it? School, I mean?"

"As much as any kid, I guess," he said. "She hates math, although she's pretty good at it. She likes history. Especially Egyptian history. Give her a book about Pharaohs and mummies and pyramids, and she'll read it, cover to cover." He reached for a tool from the toolbox and leaned over the engine. "'Course, she could be an honor student if she wanted to be..."

Tess moved closer, until she shared the cool shade of the tree with him.

"She's just decided she doesn't want to be."

An unwitting frown creased her brow as she placed her hands on the fender of the car and leaned forward an inch. What he said about their daughter bothered her.

Erin was only ten years old. Much too young to realize the value of a good education. Tess remembered her own goals as a youngster; to postpone or skirt altogether any and all schoolwork she could. The only thing on a child's mind is playtime. Having fun with friends and talking on the telephone took precedence over everything and anything.

Her memory of Mr. Fieldman was crystal clear. Her fifth-grade teacher had threatened to hold her back a year. She'd been mortified at the thought of being left behind by her friends. But worse, her father had been terribly upset. He'd taken away her telephone privileges for two full months until her next report card had proven that she'd gotten her grades back on track.

She blinked, studying Dylan's profile. She didn't understand how he could be content to allow Erin to choose her own achievement level. Was he doing all he could as a parent to see to it that Erin got the best education possible? Tess's chest pinched painfully when she remembered all her own father had done, all he'd sacrificed, so that she could become a doctor.

However, following close on the heels of grief was an underlying anger that smothered everything else when she remembered that her father had sold her baby girl, had cost her all those years with Erin. It was difficult for her to comprehend how she could still love her dad, still grieve for him, now that she knew what he'd done. She pushed the confusing thoughts aside.

"Erin will turn things around," Dylan commented. "She'll realize how important school is before too much longer. She'll come to understand what's best for her."

Maybe when she's thirty, Tess mused silently. Knowing what was truly best simply wasn't in a child's nature. Getting what was wanted was the number one priority.

But then, what made her an expert? What did she know about children? Only what she remembered from her own childhood. And who was she to come traipsing into Pine Meadow and start telling Dylan how he should or shouldn't raise Erin? However, if she didn't speak her mind, if she didn't tell Dylan that she felt he ought to put a little pressure on their daughter regarding her schooling, what kind of mother did that make her?

Lord, this was so complicated. She decided it was best to leave it alone now. To wait until she had more information before she butted heads with him over this. She'd be meeting Erin this afternoon. Maybe then she'd have more facts on which to base her assumptions regarding Dylan's skills as a father.

Hoping to steer the conversation to safer ground, she queried, "Does Erin play a musical instrument? I played the flute when I was in grade school." A smile lingered on her lips. "I sang in the choir, too."

"She's not in the band," Dylan said, pulling out a spark plug from its slot. "She's not in the choir, either." Then he said, "Hand me the spark plug gauge out of the toolbox, would you?"

Automatically she picked up the circular metal disk with two manicured fingers. It was dull and dark with years of greasy use. She held it out to him.

"It's round," he told her, his attention still on the engine. "A little larger than a half dollar—"

He turned his face toward her then, saw that she'd already picked it up. A spontaneous chuckle of delight escaped from her when she saw the utter surprise registered in his eyes.

"I must have handed you this thing about a million times," she reminded him.

One corner of his mouth hitched up with the memory. "Yeah," he said softly, "I guess you did at that."

His smile was sexy enough to cause her blood to heat in her veins. He took the gauge from her, his fingers lightly brushing hers, and a strangely familiar hum vibrated across her skin, like a warm, exotic breeze on bare flesh. She successfully quelled the sharp inhalation of surprise and pure pleasure that welled up within her. Dylan turned back to his work, and Tess was left wondering if he'd felt the sensual buzz that had shivered between them.

Dylan glanced up at her, his eyes barely lighting on

hers before he busied himself with the plug. But in that instant, she recognized awareness in his green gaze. He was conscious of the insistent pulse resonating between them. She was positively certain of it.

Her heart raced and perspiration prickled her brow even though the promise of autumn injected a crisp edge into the air. Her inward reactions to this...this *magnetism* were quite involuntary, and she was helpless against them. The increased heart rate, the elevated blood pressure, the feeling of pins and needles prickling every inch of her skin. She could do nothing to fight these physical responses to Dylan. But that didn't mean she had to give in to them, or let him see what he was doing to her.

Knowing he, too, was aware of the intense humming, and that if he wasn't battling the same corporal reactions, he was at least feeling discomfited by the awkwardness, she decided to do them both a favor and offer up a topic of conversation. If nothing else, it would take their minds off what they were feeling.

"Nice car." She was happy that her offhand remark sounded so sincere since her brain was in utter chaos with all the bells and whistles clanging in alarm as adrenaline and hormones surged through her body at dizzying speeds.

She saw the muscles in his shoulders visibly relax, distinct evidence that he was relieved that she wanted to snuff out—or at least ignore—the strong attraction hovering, thick and viscous as a heavy fog.

"Thanks," he murmured, not looking up.

She knew he was avoiding her eyes, avoiding her face. Avoiding the enticement that swirled around them under that tree. Her gaze riveted to his back. And she felt a deep disappointment when she realized that, rather than lessening the tension coiling inside her, seeing the tautness of his muscles release only heightened the emotions. She wanted to reach out and run her fingertips across his bulky shoulders. But she was able to elude the urge. Just barely.

Mild panic set in, and she felt impelled to save herself, to save the both of them. From what, she hadn't a clue.

Stepping away from the car, away from *him,* she looked down the length of the shiny auto. She hadn't even noticed it until now. Before this moment, Dylan had taken up every thought in her head. Well, maybe not every thought. A few of them had focused on Erin.

But now her breath left her in a gush of admiration.

"This isn't simply a nice car," she amended, awe unmistakable in her voice. "It's a *beautiful* car."

"Thanks," Dylan said again. He tossed the spark plug gauge back into the toolbox, his upper body disappearing under the hood. "It's a '36 roadster. Erin and I built it from the ground up."

The socket wrench clicked as Dylan screwed the plug into place.

"Erin helped you?"

"Mm-hmm," he said.

Studying the shiny, canary-yellow paint, she wryly commented, "I'd have taken you for a candy-apple-red kinda guy."

He chuckled. "Erin picked out the color." He peered from around the hood, caught her gaze. "I did vote for red, actually. But Erin talked me out of it."

As they looked at each other, the mesmerizing attraction that charged the air made them self-conscious and his eyes shadowed over.

She blurted, "And Erin actually helped you build

it, huh?'' Despite the massive, distracting awkwardness, Tess felt proud of her daughter.

''Yes,'' he told her, bending to work on the engine. ''This is what takes up all our extra time. This is the reason why she doesn't play the flute. Or sing in the choir.'' His tone grew more muffled as he gruffly added, ''Or take ballet lessons. Or piano lessons.''

What was that she heard in his tone? Bitterness? Resentment? Regret? She was about to ask him when a young mechanic rounded the building, calling Dylan's name.

''Yeah?'' Immediately Dylan reached for the ever-present rag in his back pocket and began wiping off his fingers.

''The school nurse just called,'' he told Dylan. ''Erin's sick. Upchucked her breakfast. She needs to come home.''

Concern bit into Tess's brow, made her feel suddenly anxious. Her stomach felt jittery, as it did when she'd worked her stint in the ER. Only now, she couldn't seem to get the feeling under control. She couldn't seem to keep the shakiness at bay, or keep it from affecting her thought processes.

''Thanks, Dave,'' Dylan said. ''Can you hold down the fort until I get back?''

''Sure,'' the young man said.

Dylan listed specific instructions regarding several automobiles, but Tess was too intent on thoughts of Erin to hear clearly.

The anxiety flooding her mind was…odd. Her career as a medical practitioner brought her into daily contact with sick people. But she never experienced this panicky apprehension that ate at her right now. Calm, cool logic was her best asset as a doctor. However, the distress she was feeling seemed almost... unmanageable. She *wanted* to pay attention to what Dylan was saying, she *wanted* to find out more about what the school nurse might have said, but this strange frantic worry caught her in a grip she couldn't break.

Suddenly it came to her that this unfamiliar panic was stemming from her maternal side. Her mothering instincts. Up until this moment, Tess hadn't even realized she had any.

But then, she thought, wasn't it maternal concern that had her wanting Erin to try hard to achieve great things in regards to her education? She was certain it was. And the pride she'd felt when Dylan revealed that their daughter was actually helping him build this hot rod. That, too, was part of her motherly nature. This revelation was nice, but worry over Erin crowded out everything else.

"Dylan," she said.

He turned to face her.

"Is it all right if I go along with you?"

The question was coated with a heavy layer of concern, and Dylan evidently noticed it.

"Sure," he said. "Don't worry. She's okay. But I do need to get cleaned up just a little before we go. Let's go into my office and you can wait for me there."

As they rounded the building, Tess couldn't help but marvel at how relaxed he was. If he was worried about Erin, he was hiding it pretty well.

"How can you be sure?" Her query slipped from her lips before she even had time to think about it. "That she's okay, I mean."

"If it was a real emergency," Dylan said, entering

one of the shop's big bay doors, "the principal would have called. And she wouldn't have passed a message through Dave. She'd have asked for me directly."

"Oh." There must have been curiosity in her tone, because he continued to elaborate how he knew the procedure.

"Erin fell on the playground when she was in second grade," he told her. "She hit her head and had a pretty good gash that needed stitches, and that meant a trip to the emergency room." He grinned at her. "The principal called me."

Tess nodded, feeling a little more assured that Erin wasn't too bad off.

"Besides," Dylan continued, "I'm fairly sure I know what's wrong with her."

By this time, they were in his office, and she simply raised her brows and waited. He smiled at her, and every muscle in her body seemed to petrify at the sexy sight. The years had done nothing except make him more handsome than she could ever have imagined, and that was an incredible idea seeing as she'd felt he was simply to-die-for gorgeous when she'd been a teen. It became difficult to inhale, like all the oxygen in the air suddenly congealed into a thick, gelatinous mass.

"It's you."

There was no censure in his tone. But then she was too concerned with garnering control over her breathing and her erratic heartbeat caused by that too-charming grin of his to pay too much attention to what was being expressed in his voice.

"I'm sure Erin has turned herself inside out just thinking about meeting you today after school."

His smile widened and Tess was sure her knees

were going to fail her terribly and buckle under her. Shakily she eased herself down onto the armrest of the couch. Why did he have to be so darned good-looking? And why couldn't she seem to focus more of her energy on churning up those maternal worries?

It seemed that once Dylan had assured her that Erin was okay, that she wasn't in the throes of some violent illness, the motherly panic Tess had experienced had subsided and she'd become utterly transfixed by Dylan's handsome face, his clear green gaze and that seductive smile. That hum of attraction was back, full force.

"I think it will be best for Erin—"

Dylan continued to talk as though he was completely unaware of the effect he was having on her. For that, Tess was thankful.

"—if we got this first meeting over with between you two."

Her eyes were glued to his, and she couldn't seem to summon any sort of facial expression to save her soul. She was a mass of raw, pulsing nerves, aware of his every breath, his every move. All at once, he seemed to sense the tension she was feeling.

"Does that sound like a good idea to you?" His tone was soft, almost curious.

She couldn't get her tongue to form words, and she sat there feeling like a mute idiot.

"Tess?"

Speak, damn it! she silently commanded. Say something. Anything! Desperation built in the pit of her stomach, and Tess felt it roil there. It churned in a bubbling frenzy until it was strong enough to kick her into action.

"Sure." Her answer finally burst from her in a

breathy whisper. And she prayed he didn't expect anything more from her at the moment.

"Great," he said. "Let me clean up a bit and we'll take off."

Dylan disappeared into the adjoining rest room and closed the door. Tess was only vaguely conscious of hearing water run as she berated herself for allowing this...this mesmerizing force, or whatever it was called, to totally hypnotize her into this absolutely imbecilic, stupefied state. She had to snap out of it. She couldn't function like this. It was ridiculous.

Okay, so Dylan was good-looking. So what? She had met good-looking men before. She had learned beside them, worked with them, every day.

But none of them were Dylan, a tiny voice silently pointed out.

Tess gulped air into her lungs. She stood up and paced to the window. She still felt a little shaky, but—she inhaled deeply again—she could ignore this attraction she was feeling. If she tried hard enough.

Water droplets glistened in his neatly combed hair, his hands and face freshly washed when he stepped from the rest room. He was drying his hands on a navy towel.

"I'm just about ready," he told her.

She tugged her long purse strap back up onto her shoulder. "Me, too," she said.

"Wait."

She froze as he approached her. He reached out and gingerly took her fingers away from the leather strap. His skin was warm and ever-so-slightly damp, and she detected the lemony aroma of soap.

"You're dirty," he said, gently wiping her fingertips with the towel. "That gauge you handed me must have been grimy. You'll get grease on your clothes, if you're not careful.''

He was so close. Too close. The lemon scent of the soap couldn't hide the darkly sensuous aroma of his cologne, a fragrance that brought to mind hot, tropical nights spent in the arms of a lover.

She should step away from him, make it perfectly clear that she was quite capable of taking care of her own hygiene. But she didn't move. Didn't breathe.

''There,'' he said. ''That's much better.''

But he didn't release her fingers from his grasp. Helplessly her eyes were drawn to his face. The curve of his jaw, the slight crook of his nose that she knew had been caused by a particularly rough football tackle in high school, that green gaze that was intense with emotion.

It would be so easy to lean toward him. It would only take a tiny movement on her part, to give him the signal he seemed to be seeking. But she remained stubbornly still.

Finally he said, ''Let's go. We'll take my car.'' And he started for the door.

Tess gave herself a moment. Waited a second or two for the haze in her head to clear.

You fool, her brain barked at her, *he wasn't looking for any signal. You're conjuring up a fine figment in that wild imagination of yours.*

But as she walked out into the shop, she knew in her heart that she wasn't a fool.

Chapter Six

The school building was the same one Tess had attended as an elementary student. The parking lot had been enlarged and new equipment had been added to the playground, but for the most part, not much more than that had changed over the years.

Dylan hadn't said two words during the five-minute ride to the school. The awkwardness hovered, just waiting to swamp them. They were both doing their best to ignore it.

He paused at the door, allowing her to enter into the foyer first.

"Do you think she'll be in the principal's office?" Tess asked, her excitement over actually talking to Erin mounting by the moment. "Or in the nurse's office?"

"When I've picked her up before," he said, "she was waiting in the...ah, there she is."

With a small tilt of his head, he indicated the school's main office to their immediate left. Her gaze followed his lead and came to rest on her daughter's pale face on the other side of the glass wall.

The poor child looked like an anxious bucket of nerves, her doe-eyed expression tearing at Tess's heart.

"She looks a wreck," she whispered to Dylan.

"She's okay," he told her. "She looked the same way before her first roller-coaster ride." He chuckled softly. "In fact, that's the same expression she had *during* the ride, and for about an hour after, too."

Tess realized that he was attempting to assuage the apprehension and worry she was feeling so strongly she was sure it must actually be emanating off her. But she knew nothing could calm her emotional state—nothing short of touching her daughter's face, discovering for herself that Erin really was okay.

Glancing through the glass wall again, Tess saw that Erin had become aware of her presence, the child's brown eyes growing large as they locked onto her.

"Come on," Dylan told her. "Let's put her out of her misery."

Tess stopped short, his words striking her like an unexpected snakebite. "Misery?" Why would Dylan think Erin would feel miserable about meeting her?

"Yeah," he responded, "can't you see she's dying to meet you?"

"Oh—" she nodded "—I see what you mean." So he hadn't meant the statement hurtfully. Like a busy bee discovering a pollen-coated flower, Tess's gaze lit on Erin once again. Then she urged Dylan forward. "I need to be put out of my misery, too." Her voice hushed to a whisper as she added, "Ten long years of misery."

She was only vaguely aware of the curious sidelong

glance Dylan cast her. But she didn't give it a thought because once she pushed open the office door and came face-to-face with Erin, every nuance of her attention honed in on her daughter.

Standing there speechless, Tess felt the urge to kick herself. She had no idea what she should say. What *did* a mother say to a child she'd never met? Frustration only fanned the flames of anxiety burning in the pit of her stomach.

The perfect opening line was what she should have been pondering all morning rather than allowing so much of her energy to be sapped by the mysterious and hopeless attraction she'd felt toward Dylan. Long moments seemed to tick by, even though Tess knew she'd only been in the office a few short seconds at the most. Why wasn't Dylan stepping in to ease the discomfort laying heavy around them all? Ironically it was Erin who spoke first, her tone hushed with obvious awe.

"You came."

Tess watched the child's bottom lip disappear between her teeth, astonishment clearly expressed in her wide brown gaze.

"You really came."

A lump formed in Tess's throat. *Oh, please don't cry,* she silently pleaded with herself. *Please don't make an utter fool of yourself in front of this precious child.*

Unable to find the words to speak, and afraid of what her voice would sound like even if she did, Tess simply nodded, her eyes filling with happy tears as she, too, unwittingly captured her bottom lip between her teeth.

"I'll be taking my daughter home," Dylan told the school secretary.

"Very good, Mr. Minster," the woman said, giving Tess a blatantly curious look. "Gather your things together, Erin."

After picking up her book bag, Erin lifted her hand to the secretary. "Bye, Mrs. Downham. See ya tomorrow."

"You take it easy this afternoon now." The woman addressed Erin, but her gaze was still firmly affixed to Tess.

"I will," Erin assured her.

Then the child did an extraordinary thing. She slipped her hand into Tess's and said, "Come on, Mom. Let's go."

Erin's intention was obvious—to proudly and prominently reveal Tess's identity to the secretary. But Tess was so overwhelmed by hearing herself referred to as Mom, she didn't have enough of her wits about her to notice just how the elderly lady behind the big desk responded.

Mom. Her daughter had called her *Mom.* A brand-new lump of emotion welled in her throat, larger than the first. Tess found it hard to swallow, hard to breathe.

Erin held on to her hand all the way out to the car. Tess experienced a state of utter euphoria that was overwhelming. An elation that made her quite giddy. Made her actually see things in a new way. The trees surrounding the parking lot seemed to shimmer with life, their leaves a shocking and vibrant green. The clouds were larger, puffier, like huge tufts of marshmallow floating in a strikingly blue sky. And Tess knew that this new, resplendent vision was caused by the small, soft palm firmly nestled in hers.

Dylan opened first the front passenger-side door of his car, and then the back one. "All aboard," he told them.

He smiled, but Tess noticed the tension on his face, in his voice, and her joyous fog parted long enough for her to wonder what he might be thinking. However, before Tess could come to any conclusions, her daughter graced her with a large-eyed, adoring expression that was enough to take away a person's breath.

"Can I sit up front with you?" Erin asked her.

"Sure." Her answer was automatic. At that moment, she'd have agreed to ride up on top of the car's roof, if that's what her daughter would have requested.

But what if Dylan has rules about Erin riding in the front seat? The question tramped across the happy haze of her brain, and she turned a querying gaze on him.

She tried to gauge if he might be feeling that she'd overstepped her bounds, but all she saw were the same tiny lines of strain bracketing his forced smile. Maybe *that* was why he seemed so tense. Maybe he was worried she might go overboard here.

I don't plan to come between you and Erin. Her assurance to him reverberated in her head. His curt, cool response came close on its heels.

The last thing Tess wanted was for Dylan to feel threatened. She glanced down at Erin, "What I should have said was, you can sit up front if it's okay with your dad."

Dylan glowered at her over their daughter's head.

Sure, the expression that passed his features seemed to say, let *me* be the bad guy.

Tossing him an apologetic look, Tess said to Erin, "Maybe I ought to ride in the back."

"Don't be silly," Dylan said, irritation flashing in his eyes as he slammed shut the rear door. "Would the two of you just get in already?"

Erin hustled into the front seat and Tess quickly followed.

The ride home was filled with Erin's chatter. Tess never guessed so many words could be spewed from a human mouth, so many different topics touched upon, in such a short amount of time. In the fifteen minutes it took for Dylan to drive to his home, Tess found out a veritable fount of information about her daughter.

Erin's teacher's name was Mrs. Edwards, and she was the nicest teacher in the school. Last year, Erin had had the meanest witch of a teacher, a woman who had a terrible habit of tugging at her sagging stockings to the point that all the children in the school made fun of the ol' witch.

At this Dylan had spoken Erin's name in a tone of censure. Erin had absently tossed out a quick, "Sorry," and then continued down a different path.

April and Wendy, Tess learned, were Erin's two best girlfriends, and Toby was her best boyfriend. Not that Toby was her *boy*friend, Erin took great pains to stress. He was just a friend who happened to be a boy. But he was still cool, even though most boys in her class sucked because they wouldn't let the girls play basketball with them on the playground. Erin could make lots of baskets. Better than some of them, even. But Toby was okay, even though he sometimes played basketball with the other boys. Mrs. Edwards made history really fun. And she just gave the kids the coolest team assignment. They could make any kind of three-dimensional project they wanted. From history, of course. And Erin had teamed up with Toby and the two of them were going to make a replica of King Tutankhamen's death mask.

Did Tess know that the real death mask was twenty-one inches high and was made of gold and lapis lazuli? Lapis lazuli was a beautiful blue mineral rock. She had learned that in science. Erin didn't like science much. But last year, she and her dad had made a volcano that really erupted—an oh-so-cool oozy mixture of ketchup and sand—and she had won second place in the Science Olympiad. Next week Mrs. Edwards was taking the kids to the local fruit orchard for a tour and Erin was sure everyone would get to pick an apple. Right off the trees. At least that's what everyone thought was going to happen.

Dylan pulled into his driveway. The brick ranch house sat back from the road. Big tulip trees shaded the wide front lawn, a stock-rail fence enclosed the even larger back yard.

"Nice," she murmured.

"Hey," Erin continued to ramble, "maybe you'd like to come along."

Tess glanced down at the child. "Come along?"

"To the *orchard.* There are always a few parent chaperones when we go on trips. Bobby Taylor's mother always goes. Bobby's hyper and he's always gettin' into trouble. His mom comes so she can keep him under control. I could ask Mrs. Edwards tomorrow if there's room on the bus for you. I bet there is—"

"Whoa now," Dylan said as he cut the engine. "Slow down a little bit. You're overwhelming—"

He stopped, obviously stumped about something. Tess glanced at him curiously.

"—your mother."

The two words sounded stilted, stiff and uncomfortable as a brand-new shirt. Well, Tess decided, all of them were unaccustomed to the phrase. But she guessed they'd have to get used to using and hearing the words *Mom* and *Mother*.

After clearing his throat, Dylan continued, "Let's get inside. You need to change out of your school clothes. We'll worry about the trip later."

Evidently Erin's disappointment was sharp enough to silence her. At least for a moment or two.

They tramped around to the side of the house and entered through the door leading into the bright and airy eat-in kitchen.

"It's lovely," Tess exclaimed. "So welcoming, and open."

"Thanks," Dylan said.

"Dad built a lot of the house all by himself."

Erin's pride in her father was clearly evident in her voice, and Tess smiled.

"I woulda' helped," the child went on. "But a'course, I was too small."

Dylan placed a loving hand on Erin's shoulder. "You wield a wicked hammer," he said. "I'd have loved the help."

Erin beamed under the compliment.

"You go up and change," Dylan told her.

The child captured Tess's attention. "You wanna come see my room?"

Before Tess could respond, Dylan said, "Don't you

think it would be best if you went up and changed, and then made sure your room is picked up?''

''Aw, Dad,'' Erin complained. ''I made my bed this morning.''

''I know you did. But your pajamas were wadded in a ball by your dresser.'' Dylan planted one hand on the back of a kitchen chair. ''You should fold them up and put them away.''

''I don't know why I gotta fold 'em up,'' she muttered. ''I'm just gonna wear 'em again tonight.''

Dylan ignored her moaning. ''And what about all those stuffed animals scattered about? Don't you want your mom to see your room when it's straightened up and not—''

''Okay,'' Erin said, turning toward the hallway at the far end of the room, ''okay, already.''

Once they were alone, Dylan turned to Tess.

''Boy,'' he said, ''she gave up awfully easy.''

Tess chuckled. ''You presented a good argument.''

Now it was his turn to laugh. ''That's usually not enough with Erin.'' He looked toward the empty hallway. ''She must want to make a good impression on you.''

His head swiveled, his gaze lighting once again on Tess's face. The fatherly love she read in his eyes was appealing. Very much so. It was evident that Dylan had a deep affection for Erin, and that pleased Tess to no end.

''She's a good kid,'' he said.

Tess nodded. ''I can tell.'' After a moment, she added, ''You've done a good job of raising her.''

Then silence descended. And the good-humored camaraderie permeating the air began to metamorphose.

The change seemed to be excruciatingly slow. And just as excruciatingly noticeable.

In an effort to avoid his green gaze, she lowered her eyes—and found herself admiring the corded muscles of his forearms, studying the pattern of the dark, springy hair growth on his tanned skin, noticing the strength of his long, tapering fingers, remembering how those fingers had brought her such exquisite pleasure.

The memory of one particular night came to her, sharp, clear. The air had been hot, muggy. In an effort to cool off, she and Dylan had hopped on his motorcycle and sped out of town. He had taken her to Harrington Woods. The quiet isolation had been pure pleasure, the cool, shading trees heaven. But it was what had taken place there beneath those towering trees, what Dylan had done to her with his strong, yet gentle hands, that had her heart tripping in her chest, her breath turning shallow even now.

Stop! she told herself. Just stop.

Swallowing, she shoved the erotic memories from her. She steeled herself, and then lifted her gaze to his.

Her eyes widened. Dylan looked just as disturbed, just as caught up in the past, as she. Finally he blinked and then focused on her, his face taut. He truly seemed shaken to the core. The thick mantle of mysterious attraction had settled on them yet again. To deny it would have been foolish, and futile.

"I should go."

His voice was raw and grating. And Tess clamped her bottom lip between her teeth to keep from rushing to agree with him too quickly, knowing that to do so would have come off sounding extremely abrupt.

However, it was obvious that they both needed some space.

"I have loads of work to do at the shop," he continued. "You and Erin have ten years to catch up on. And you don't need me here while you do that. You wouldn't mind if I went back to work, would you?"

It was almost as if he were arguing with himself: the father in him wanting to be close to his daughter should she need him during what could be an emotional experience, the man in him wanting desperately to run from the sensuous dynamite threatening to explode right under his feet. Tess easily empathized with him. She felt a strong urging to flee herself.

"I wouldn't mind at all," she quietly said. But then she couldn't help pointing out the obvious. "But Erin might mind. She might mind a lot. Seeing as how the two of us have never been alone before. I don't want her to feel awkward or self-conscious."

The moment was frozen in time, as Tess and Dylan stared at each other in silence. How ironic that Tess would want Erin to avoid the very emotions she and Dylan were feeling right at this moment.

What you're feeling transcends awkwardness, surpasses self-consciousness, a voice rang in her head as loud as the peal of a bell. *What you're feeling is a drawing, a pulling, a gravitation.*

Allure. Temptation. Beguilement.

Strong words, Tess realized. Strong feelings. Feelings that were, at this very moment, putting up one heck of a battle inside her.

"Right," he said, looking around frantically for his best escape route. "You're absolutely right. I'll go talk to her."

With that said, he fled down the hallway and turned the corner out of sight.

Tess set her purse on the oak table and moved to the green-tiled island. She smoothed her fingers across the cool surface. A diversion was what she needed. Something that would take her mind off Dylan and the heady emotions swirling around them when they were together.

Glancing around her, she decided this really was a lovely room. A kitchen a woman would enjoy cooking in, entertaining in, planning meals that would lovingly nourish her happy family.

Her chin tipped up, and she felt a frown bite deeply into her brow. Where had that thought come from? she wondered. She wasn't one to think about hearth and home. When Dylan had rejected her, and then only months later she'd lost her child, Tess had pretty much decided having a family wasn't for her. The decision hadn't been a conscious one—she'd just resolved that love simply hurt too much. So she'd locked up her heart. And focused on her studies. Consequently she had been a damn good medical student, graduating in the top ten percent of her class. She could have specialized, gone on to study, in-depth, any number of areas in the medical field. But she'd wanted to become a general M.D. Someone who looked after families...

The thought trailed off as questions seeped into her brain. Why had she chosen to become a *family* practitioner? Was it because she'd shut out of her life any idea of having a husband and children of her own? Had she chosen her profession—caring for parents and their offspring—in some attempt to fill some kind of void inside her?

The questions were daunting.

Dylan barreled back into the room, pulling his keys from his pocket as he came.

"Everything's all set," he told her.

Tess couldn't help but notice how he was avoiding eye contact with her.

"Erin's more than happy to stay here with you." He moved to the back door. "I'll be home a little after six, if that's okay."

Tess told him that was fine. He opened the door, and then turned back as an idea struck him.

"If you'll give me your keys," he said, "I'll have Dave drive your car over here. One of the other mechanics will follow him to bring him back to the shop. That way your car will be here if you need it."

"That would be great," she said. She went to the table, and when she reached for her purse to get her keys, Dylan actually took a backward step.

She found the keys and he took them, wordlessly, a myriad of cryptic messages expressed in his gaze. Then after giving her a quick nod, he was gone.

What the two of them were experiencing—attraction, allure, temptation—was simply too obvious to be ignored for too long. She'd tried to disregard the feelings, as she was sure Dylan had. But it wasn't working. This magnetism just seemed to grow stronger. Their feelings were going to have to be acknowledged. Talked about. Reckoned with.

Maybe by bringing their feelings out into the open, discussing them like two mature adults, the emotions could be put to rest.

But that would have to be left for some other time. For now, Tess needed to give her daughter her undivided attention.

* * *

Over the next three afternoons, Tess got a taste of what she imagined heaven must be like, and she was finding the experience to be utterly delectable. From three o'clock until six o'clock, she discovered what it meant to be a mom. Feelings blossomed inside her—maternal feelings she'd never experienced before coming home to Pine Meadow, before meeting her adorable, fun-loving, outgoing daughter. Feelings that were warm and fuzzy and...completely indescribable. If some scientist could isolate whatever chemical the brain secreted that conjured these complicated feelings—this joyous euphoria, this giddy pleasure, this intense pride—and bottle the stuff, he'd become a millionaire overnight.

Erin was intelligent and quick-witted. A joy to be around. And Tess savored those three hours she spent with her daughter every afternoon. Tess would meet Erin at the bus stop and walk with her back to Dylan's house. Usually Dylan picked up Erin and took her to the shop, but he'd agreed to allow Tess to stay with their daughter until he arrived home from work.

That very first evening, the day that she had gone to school with Dylan to pick up Erin, Tess had stayed and had dinner with the two of them. With disastrous results. The air was so awkward between Tess and Dylan that Erin had picked up on it. Misreading the tense emotions vibrating in the air as anger, Erin had asked why her parents were upset with each other. Dylan had done his best to calm her fears, but if it hadn't been for Erin's endless chatter, the meal would have been eaten in total silence.

Tess tried to snuff out the electricity that pulsed between her and Dylan, but she failed. Miserably. She knew they needed to talk about what was happening to them. And she was certain that once they did, once they acknowledged these echoes from their past attraction—at least that's how she described what she was feeling for Dylan—then they could both put all this silliness behind them. However, a private talk with Dylan was next to impossible with Erin at Tess's elbow every moment. So after that first evening, Tess avoided further awkwardness, making sure she came up with some excuse, and left the house as soon as Dylan arrived home from work around six-fifteen. But getting their feelings out in the open was inevitable.

However this Friday afternoon, Tess found herself driving down a lonely road rather than spending a few delightful hours with her daughter. Seems that Erin had to get together with Toby to work on their history project, the replica of King Tut's death mask. Although Erin was disappointed that she and Tess wouldn't have the afternoon together, Tess had also heard an underlying excitement in her daughter's voice about the project when the child called to alert her to the change of plans.

Tess slowed to a stop at a crossroads and smiled. Erin had gotten off the subject at hand during their phone conversation. As usual, Tess thought, her grin widening. Erin had told her that Toby lived on the outskirts of Harrington Woods, and then the child had launched into a detailed confabulation describing the fort she and Toby were building in one particular tree. Of course, Erin had gone on, they wouldn't have time to work on that this evening, not with their project due the middle of next week.

It was this discussion that got Tess to thinking. About Harrington Woods. About these whispers from the past that were pulling at her every single time she was with Dylan. If she were to face the past, confront the strong attraction—the powerful love—she'd felt for Dylan, then maybe she would be better able to deal with what she was feeling for him in the here and now. And what better place for such a confrontation than the spot in Harrington Woods that all those years ago they had deemed "theirs"?

No better place, she'd decided, pulling onto the shoulder of the two-lane road when she spied the overgrown dirt lane she knew had been her and Dylan's "entrance into Paradise."

"This isn't Harrington Woods," she remembered whispering into Dylan's ear one hot, sultry afternoon, "this is paradise." And from that day on, their spot had been dubbed Paradise.

It was nothing more than a dirt track now with sticker bushes standing sentinel, reaching out to snag anyone who might trespass. She didn't dare risk scratching the paint job on her car by driving down the lane. So she switched off the engine, locked the car door and carefully picked her way through the narrow opening into the woods.

Silence enveloped her. And with each step she took down the hard-packed trail, the outside world seemed to slip farther and farther away. Isolation. Solitude. Those were the very things she and Dylan had sought in coming here. Not complete isolation. But a solitude for the two of them from the rest of life. And they had found that. Time and again. Here, in this place.

It was so easy to imagine herself at sixteen and seventeen. It was so easy to conjure what she'd thought were long lost feelings of eager anticipation of being with the boy she loved. She could almost feel the wind

against her skin as she rode behind Dylan on his motorcycle. The smell of his leather jacket pungent and
heady. The strength of his broad back and thighs as
she snuggled close to him, holding on tight while they
bumped down the lane toward Paradise. Every nerve
ending in her body alert with tingling expectation and
impatience to taste his kiss, feel his hands on her skin.
Because she knew with joyous certainty that, after
talking and teasing and laughing together, they would
express their love in a most physical and intimate manner.

Tess stopped, and smiled when she found it. Paradise had changed. Just as the lane into the Harrington
Woods had become overgrown, so had Paradise. But
the felled tree that had serviced as a seat was still
there, moss and lichen covered now. As were the initials Dylan had lovingly carved into the bark of a
nearby oak. The letters had become a little distorted
by the tree's growth over the years, but Tess could
easily read them.

Sighing, she simply stood there and enjoyed the se-
renity; the vibrant greens in so many different shades,
the rustling of the slight breeze through the leaves
overhead, the scurrying of some unseen squirrel or
chipmunk. She blinked, turning her head to look toward where she'd come from, when a different sound
broke the tranquil atmosphere—

The distinct *pug, pug, pug* of an approaching motorcycle.

Chapter Seven

She should have felt panicked when he appeared. She should have gasped. Looked for a place to hide. The least she should have done was feel surprised. But she wasn't any of these things. In fact, his showing up here—*now*—in Paradise seemed to be the most natural thing in the world.

He cut the engine, pulled off his helmet, ran his fingers through his dark hair. Tess did the only thing she could do—she offered him a welcoming smile. A smile he returned. And immediately she was aware that every bit of the stifling awkwardness she had felt between them since she'd returned to Pine Meadow was gone. Dissolved into thin air.

Tess knew without any doubt that the location was the cause. Paradise was, simply put, a magical place. A place where nothing bad could ever happen. A place where dreams came to fruition. A place of unending happiness...no matter what might be happening ''out there'' in the real world.

"Hello," she said.

His soft smile widened in silent greeting.

"I dropped Erin off at Toby's and saw your car parked along the side road," he said, explaining his presence.

But Tess chose to believe that it was fate that sent him here. That enchanted explanation fitted the moment much better. At least, it did in her mind.

"I was headed back to the shop," he told her. "But then I spotted your car." He expelled a short, quick exhalation that was filled with irony. "It was almost as if my bike was headed down the path before I even had a chance to think about turning."

This admission only added to the mystical quality of the moment, only increased her certainty that destiny had stepped into this situation.

Dylan lowered the kickstand and lifted himself off the motorcycle. Then he set his helmet on the black leather seat.

"It's been a long time," he said as he approached her.

Watching him gaze around at Paradise, Tess sensed the awe he was feeling, saw the memories churning in his head through the windows of his clear, green eyes. She understood completely, because she felt awed herself.

"Yes" was all she said, the overwhelming mesmerism of the situation, of the place, forcing her voice to a mere whisper.

His tone, too, was hushed, when, after a moment, he said, "What would have possessed us to—"

His sentence was cut short, his face actually tingeing with embarrassed color. Tess shook her head, unable to stop the disconcerted grin that pulled and then lingered at one corner of her mouth. She knew exactly what he was thinking. To what he was referring. In a moment of boldness, she decided to finish his thought.

"Completely unclothe in the wide-open spaces of Harrington Woods?" she supplied.

They looked at each other in total silence. And then finally they burst out laughing until they were both teary-eyed.

"Teenagers can be very..." This time she was the one finding it difficult to voice what was on her mind.

"Uninhibited?" he offered.

Again they shared a chuckle, this one smaller, less sheepish and more...intimate.

She looked around at the trails. "It's a wonder we weren't ever, ah, interrupted. By hikers, or people out looking for a quiet picnic spot. Or the park ranger, even. We were awfully lucky, wouldn't you say?"

"Well, we were either very lucky," he said, "Or someone's erotic entertainment."

Tess gasped, horrified by the mere idea of being spied upon in compromising circumstances. "Don't say that!"

Dylan laughed at her. But she wasn't upset. In fact, she found his spontaneity quite appealing.

Suddenly he fell silent. Then he said, "Wow, would you look at that."

He was studying a spot on the oak tree, the carving of their initials.

"Yes—" Tess went to the tree, reached up and traced the letters with her fingertip "—it's still here after all these years." She smiled softly, not feeling the least bit self-conscious as she read, "D. M. loves T. G. 4-ever."

Before she realized it, he'd come up behind her. So

close, she could feel his warm breath brush the side of her face, feel the solid mass of his body, not touching her, but only a fraction of an inch away.

She'd meant to come to Harrington Woods to face the demons of her past. To confront the bygone love she'd felt for Dylan, so that she could put to rest this silly attraction of the present she was feeling for him. But at this moment, in this place, the hypnotic allure that enthralled her seemed anything but silly. It seemed real. It seemed honest. It *was* honest. And had nothing whatsoever to do with the past.

"It was true, you know," he said against her ear. He placed his hand on her shoulder. "I loved you with every fiber of my being."

The magnitude of this confession wasn't lost on her. When most young men his age—eighteen and nineteen years old—had been driven by their hormones to see with just how many girls they could score, Dylan had pledged himself to her. Wholly. Completely.

"I know." She closed her eyes. Reveled in the heated male scent of him. Relished the feel of his touch. Marveled at how the very air seemed to come alive all around them.

Tess recognized his affirmation was offered as a means to assure her of his feelings at the time they had made love as teens here in Paradise. She'd been aware of his feelings then.

"I know you did," she repeated.

She turned to face him and then leaned her back against the rough bark of the oak, instinctively knowing he would close the gap between them. And he did.

"I never doubted it," she said, gazing into his gorgeous emerald eyes. Those eyes that had always had such power over her.

Her last statement wasn't the complete truth. In the end she had doubted him. With very good reason. But now wasn't the time to remember old hurts, it was a time to reminisce about—*to give tribute to*—all the wonderful times they had shared together. And there had been many.

He stroked the length of her cheek with the back of his index finger, his touch featherlight, and Tess surrendered to the urge to tilt her head and close her eyes. And then she did the most incredible thing. She reached up, took his hand in both of hers and pressed the backs of his fingers to her lips. And with his hand still captured in hers, she opened her eyes and stared directly into his gaze.

She paused, waiting to be swamped by a wave of embarrassment. But embarrassment didn't come, and she suspected that was all due to Dylan's reaction to her startlingly sensuous behavior. From the look in his eyes, one would be led to believe that what she'd done was utterly normal. Completely natural and expected.

He leaned close, his nose lightly brushing her jaw, and then her cheekbone, as he slid his fingers around her delicate throat. It wasn't a threatening motion in any way. No, it was more like he needed to feel her bare flesh against his, and her neck was all that was available to him. Instinctively her hands went to his shirtfront, her fingers splaying across the broad expanse of his chest. Lord, he felt so good, so strong, under her palms.

"You're quite a woman, Tess," he whispered. "The years have made you...beautiful."

His compliment made her feel shy. The passing years *had* changed her. And she was never more conscious of the changes as she was right now. The tiny lines fanning the corners of her eyes, the extra weight on her hips, the stray gray hair, here and there, she was so intent upon plucking. Beautiful was not a word she'd use to describe herself. But hearing him call her that made her feel…as tingly as a teenager on her first real date.

"So beautiful," he murmured against her ear.

Her body seemed to rouse from some kind of coma—as if it had been forced into some magical sleep and was being reawakened after many long years. Her heart pounded. Her blood pulsed. Her stomach danced. Her nerves prickled. Every inch of her skin was alert and waiting. Waiting for his touch. His kiss.

He pressed his nose into her hair and then against her neck, and she could hear him inhale gently, slowly, fully.

"You *smell* beautiful."

His palms smoothed over her shoulders and down her arms, lightly grazed the sides of her elbows, the backs of her fingers, all the way down to the very tips. Finally he settled his hands snugly on her hips.

"You *feel* beautiful."

A need sprouted to life within her. A need that took root in the form of a warm pulse deep inside the very core of her being. Her throat felt so dry that it ached. All she wanted was to feel his hands on her bare skin again, feel his mouth against hers.

Lifting his head, he looked into her eyes. "You *look* beautiful."

The hunger in his gaze fed her growing need until it throbbed with scorching heat.

Tess realized there remained one relevant sensation on which he could comment—*the sense of taste.* Lord, if he didn't kiss her this very moment, she'd surely go insane.

As if reading her thoughts, he lowered his head and planted on her lips the lightest of kisses. He gave one corner of her mouth an identical butterfly-kiss, then gifted the other corner with yet another.

Like the rapid growth of a leafy vine, the need in her curled with delicious heat, extending itself into every nook, every cranny inside her, until the hot pulsation was her only focus, her only concern.

Nourishing this uncontrollable need became a sudden, monumental obsession. Dylan's gossamer kisses were nice, tantalizingly so, but they were nowhere near substantial enough to satisfy the immense desire his nearness, his touch, conjured in her.

"Honey sweet," he said, the obvious desire he felt ripping his tone into jagged edges. "Even better than I remember."

How would he know? she wondered almost sulkily. How could he know what she tasted like when his mouth had barely brushed hers? What he needed was a *real* kiss, she decided. Some sultry, steamy contact that would leave no doubt in his mind as to what she tasted like.

She lifted her hands, framed his face with them, and said, "Here." And then more urgently, "Come here."

Her assertiveness evidently surprised him, for his eyes widened a fraction when she spoke. But she didn't dwell on his reaction for long, the need inside her forcing her to act, and she drew his mouth to hers.

His lips were firm and warm and moist, and she ran her tongue across them, ever so lightly, in a silent request for entry. A request he granted.

She slid her arms around his body, up along the

hard muscles of his back, and hugged him to her. Her nipples budded to life, hard as stone, as her breasts were crushed against his chest.

Their tongues danced, languidly. Hands smoothed. Fingers kneaded. Muscles bunched. And relaxed.

The sound of their breathing became audible, even frantic, as their heightened excitement caused their hearts to pound furiously, caused their bodies to demand more oxygen. She heard his ragged inhalations, and she found the sound so erotic that the need in her grew even more insatiable.

Skin. She had to feel his bare flesh against hers. Now.

Mindlessly she tugged the tail of his shirt from where it had been tucked in the waistband of his jeans. Reaching beneath it, she placed the flat of both hands against his bare back and slowly roved.

His kiss wandered then, from her lips, to her jaw, to her neck. He kissed the length of it, down, and then up again, nipping the outer edge of her ear between his teeth.

"You taste like heaven."

There was something in his voice, some delirious quality she heard, that made her smile with satisfaction and a pleasure that was so pure she felt it all the way to the tips of her toes. She dragged her hands around his waist, settling them under his shirtfront on the rippled hills and valleys of his taut stomach muscles. His breath caught sexily, and he reached to press his palm against the back of her hand, the fabric of his clothing a thin, separating barrier.

"You keep touching me like this," he said, his voice scratchy with emotion, "and you're going to drive me crazy."

Tess was amazed that their thoughts were so in tune. Her contented smile widened, and their gazes locked.

Apparently he took her silent response as some sort of invitation, for he ever so slowly reached for the bottommost button of her blouse. He released it, and then moved to the next, never breaking eye contact with her.

Tess thought her heart couldn't possibly beat any faster, nor her blood pump any hotter, but the mere anticipation of feeling his hands on her body sent her entire system into chaotic overdrive. Her own breathing became as rough as his. Her knees felt wobbly and she was relieved to have the solid old oak tree behind her for support.

Only when he'd unfastened the last button and gently folded back the facings of her blouse did his eyes stray from hers. His gaze lowered with excruciating slowness to her chest, and she watched as longing darkened his eyes to a deep hunter green.

He whispered her name and at the same time slid his hands under her breasts, capturing the weight of them in his palms. She felt the warmth of his skin through the lacy fabric of her flesh-colored bra and thought that surely she would faint dead away from the sheer pleasure of his touch. Leaning her head back against the oak tree, she closed her eyes and basked in the heat of the passionate fire he stirred in her.

She sensed him lowering his head, felt him press a hot, moist kiss on her left breast, and she could no more have suppressed the gasp that escaped her than she could have stopped the change of the seasons or the rising of the sun and moon. He leaned forward, his thighs on her thighs, and he exhaled, grinding his hips into her. The hot hardness of his desire pressed against her lower abdomen and Tess curled her fingers, gently raking her nails up the length of his back.

His spine arched and again he murmured her name. Then he crushed his mouth against hers in a kiss that bordered on savage. But it was just what Tess wanted. Just what she needed.

Their fingers became frantic as they plucked at each other's clothing; Tess trying to unbutton his shirt, he trying to unfasten her bra and slide it and her blouse off her shoulders.

A horn sounded. A loud horn. The horn of a huge sixteen-wheeler.

Dylan and Tess both started, their heads turning toward the direction of the highway, their hands still, their eyes wide with astonishment. But all they saw were green trees in the late afternoon, all they heard were birds singing overhead. They looked at one another. Stared. Searched each other's hungry-yet-uncertain gazes. Dylan was the first to break the silence.

"There was a time," he said, "when we'd never have let the sounds of traffic stop us."

"I remember." She tried hard to hold on to the delectable haze swarming around them, a sensuous fog she was reluctant to disturb.

"I guess the years have made us a little more self-conscious."

She had to smile. "A little more inhibited?"

It was a rhetorical question, as he evidently understood.

His hands slid to her waist, and after a long silence, he asked, "What are we doing, Tess?"

She closed her eyes. If he wasn't careful, his words were going to dissolve the sexy vapor that enveloped them, the way the sun burned off the haze of morning. She drew her bottom lip between her teeth for a moment, then opened her eyes to look at him. "I don't know. I don't want to think about it."

"Don't you think we should?"

Questions. Why was he asking such complicated questions? Couldn't he just enjoy the moment? Couldn't he just allow them to get caught up in the magic of this place?

They *had* gotten caught up in the magic of Paradise, she realized. *And they shouldn't have.* The thought was like a dash of icy water on hot skin.

She shifted her weight, and he stepped away from her. Immediately she comprehended the enormous mistake she'd just missed making, and the person with whom she'd just missed making it.

Tess would have made love right here on the ground. Among the weeds, the undergrowth, the poison ivy. No questions asked. She'd have given her body to Dylan. A man she didn't even know, really. A man she suspected of robbing her of the most important thing in a woman's life...her child.

What the hell was the matter with her? How could she have let her physical emotions, her sexual desires, override her logical thinking? It was ludicrous. It was inexcusable.

"You're absolutely right," she murmured, suddenly unable to look him in the face as she fumbled to dress herself. "Absolutely right."

Absently he stuffed his shirttail into his jeans. "We need to talk about this, Tess."

"I know we do. But not right now." The mere suggestion of talking about what had just taken place between them mortified her.

"But don't you think now would be the perfect time—"

"Please, Dylan! Can't you see I'm...*embarrassed?*"

He frowned. His voice was gentle as he said, "But you're not the only one to blame here. I'm just as much an adult as you. I let things get out of hand, too. I made a conscious decision to—"

"Not now!" she begged. Then she whispered, *"Please."*

She turned her back on him, flattening her hand against the rough bark of the tree, wishing she could just disappear.

Dr. Tess Galloway, educated woman, medical practitioner, unable to control her libido. Unable to restrain her sexual cravings for a man who might have done her horribly wrong. She was ashamed of herself. Of her behavior.

"We'll talk," she promised. "Some other time. I need to be alone right now. I need to get myself under control."

He sighed, but he said nothing more.

After a moment, she heard him move away from her, heard him strap on his helmet, heard the engine of his bike come to life. And soon, the sound of his motorcycle was disappearing down the trail.

Tess looked down the length of her; the buttons of her blouse fastened wrong, the fabric wrinkled, her flesh still clamoring with shameful lust. She felt totally betrayed. Not by Dylan. But by her own body. She closed her eyes, clenched her fists, hung her head, and silently berated herself with all manner of wicked words.

* * *

Tess pulled into Dylan's driveway, grinning at how her daughter danced a merry jig and waved a hearty hello at her. She'd accepted Erin's invitation to a Saturday afternoon picnic even though she felt more than a small twinge of trepidation over seeing Dylan for the first time since they had shared a kiss in Paradise.

Really, she silently scolded herself, don't you think what the two of you shared was a little more than a kiss? What with both of you so ardent in your passions? So disheveled when the episode was cut short?

Ignoring the irritating questions, Tess called out a greeting to her daughter as she exited her car.

"Cake!" Erin squealed with glee.

"It's not homemade," Tess apologized. "I bought it. My hotel room didn't come equipped with a kitchen."

"Mmm, coconut," her daughter remarked, leaning close to sniff the confection. "Chocolate's my favorite. But coconut runs a close second."

Tess smiled warmly. "Good. I'm glad my contribution to lunch will be appreciated."

"Oh, yes. Yummy!" Then Erin trotted over to where her dad was working on the yellow roadster under the shade tree. "Dad and I took Bessie out for a ride this morning," she said to Tess. "And now we're giving her a good wax job."

"Ah," Tess said, very aware that Dylan hadn't greeted her, that he hadn't even looked up, "so the car has a name."

"Yep," Erin said. "And I christened her, didn't I, Dad?"

Only when Dylan had been addressed directly did he stop rubbing the car's hood in a circular motion.

He straightened his spine, turned his eyes on his daughter. "You sure did," he said.

"Mom brought a cake," Erin told him.

Tess nearly smiled at the unspoken admonishment in her daughter's tone. Erin seemed to be urging her father to use better manners.

"I see," Dylan said. "It looks good. Delicious."

Their gazes caught and held when he spoke. Tess immediately remembered that he'd used that very word just yesterday when he'd described how she tasted to him. She felt her face flame.

Dylan then addressed Erin. "Why don't you take the cake inside? Put it on the counter in the kitchen, and we'll cut it after we eat."

"Okay."

Erin took the cake from her mother and trooped toward the side door of the house.

"You're late," Dylan said when their daughter was out of earshot. "I was beginning to think you weren't coming. I was afraid Erin was going to be disappointed."

"I'd never disappoint Erin," she said. "Never."

No matter how awkward things are between us. The unspoken words hung heavy in the air.

Dylan finally said, "Good. I'm glad to hear you say that."

His tone, along with his accusation, had Tess feeling defensive.

"I'm late because I had to stop at the bakery in town," she told him. "They were busy. And then I had a hard time deciding what I should bring."

"Well," he commented levelly, "you made a perfect choice. Like Erin said, she loves coconut. So do I."

I didn't bring it for you. The snippy retort was on the tip of her tongue, but she restrained it. Because it would have been a bold-faced lie. Yes, she had hoped her daughter would like the dessert she'd chosen, but she couldn't deny the fact that she'd hoped to please Dylan as well.

Once again, her darned emotions were in turmoil. She felt defensive at his suggestion that she might disappoint Erin. And now she felt pleased by his compliment. Lord, the man wasn't happy unless he had her feelings in total chaos.

Inadvertently her gaze dropped to his chest, to the three buttons of his cotton Henley...three unfastened buttons that exposed a small V of springy, dark chest hair. She realized this was the first time she'd seen him in anything other than his blue uniform shirt. He looked good. Very good.

Stop! she ordered herself silently. Just stop.

Dragging her gaze back to his, she nearly gasped when she saw the expression on his handsome face. He knew! He knew that she found him attractive.

Don't be a moron! her brain raged. Of course, he knew. How could he not, after that steamy kiss the two of you shared yesterday?

Anger at herself puffed up inside her. How could she be attracted to a man who might have betrayed her? She had to tell him. Today. That nothing like that...that sexy episode in Paradise could ever happen again.

The atmosphere on that bright autumn day grew more awkward by the moment. Tess opened her mouth to speak, but at that moment Erin came bursting from around the corner of the house.

"So—" Erin started talking before she was even

halfway across the lawn ''—what do you think of Bessie? Isn't she great?''

Tess nodded enthusiastically. ''She sure is. Your dad told me that you helped build the car.''

''I did.'' Erin's chest puffed with pride. ''Dad let me make lots of decisions about Bessie, too. It was my idea to have wide whites all around.''

''Wide whites all around?''

''The tires,'' Dylan explained. '''Wide whites' means the tires have extra-wide whitewalls.''

Tess noticed how little of the outside walls of the tires were black. The tires were different from any she'd seen before. But then, she wasn't in the habit of inspecting hot rods up close, either.

''And 'all around' means all the way around the car,'' Erin piped up. ''As in all four tires as opposed to just the front two.''

''Ah, I see,'' Tess said. ''They really are sharp looking.''

Erin's smile was nothing less than glorious. ''Thanks. But the best part is the engine. It's a 454 BBC crate motor with a huffer and NOS injection.''

Hearing the technical jargon spewing from her ten-year-old daughter had Tess's eyes widening in surprise. Looking over to Dylan, Tess said, ''Could you explain all that in layman's terms for me?''

Dylan's green eyes glittered with merriment. ''A *454*…as in cubic inches. *BBC* stands for Big Block Chevrolet. And *crate* means the motor was factory produced and shipped in a crate.''

''Ah…'' Tess nodded. ''That one is easy enough to understand.''

He grinned. ''Huffer means the engine has a supercharger that compresses the fuel and air mixture. It produces more horsepower. And the NOS is a system that sprays nitrous-oxide gas into the intake of the engine. Again, for more horsepower.''

Meaning to impress Erin with what little she did know about cars, Tess pointed to the tailpipe and commented, ''Bessie's got dual exhaust.''

''Actually,'' Erin said, ''the exhaust system is set up with block hugger SS headers running into—''

''Okay, okay.'' Tess laughed. ''Enough of the technical stuff. It's a foreign language to me. But I guess it all adds up to speed, right?'' She looked at Dylan. ''Bessie goes fast.''

''In the easiest of layman's terms, yes,'' Dylan said, and then he laughed.

The sound of his laughter made her heart hitch behind her ribs. She wished she had a logical explanation for her attraction to this man. She'd have thought that after all these years, his appeal to her would have waned. But as she stood there, her palms clammy, her pulse racing as fast as Bessie's state-of-the-art engine from simply listening to him laugh, Tess knew the opposite was the truth.

As usual, Erin's gears shifted swiftly when she changed the topic of the conversation by saying, ''Ya gotta come inside. To my room. I want you to see the death mask.''

Excitement glittered in Erin's eyes, and seeing it was enough to erase all the confusion swimming around in Tess's head.

''Me and Toby are almost done,'' Erin said.

''Toby and I are almost finished.'' Dylan's correction came automatically.

The child glanced up at her father's face, confusion

knitting her brow as she shrugged. "That's what I said."

Dylan's brows shot up wryly. "Not quite."

Tess chuckled. "I'd love to see the mask, honey. But maybe your dad needs help preparing lunch."

"I'm almost finished here," Dylan said, indicating the polish job he was giving the car. "And then I'll fire up the grill. I thought we'd enjoy the weather and eat outside."

"That would be nice," Tess responded.

"It'll be thirty minutes or so before the coals are ready," he continued. "You and Erin can spend some time together."

Erin took Tess by the hand. "Come on," she said, tugging Tess toward the house.

"I'm coming, I'm coming." Tess laughed. "Impatient little thing, aren't you?"

She marveled at how Erin could turn the gray clouds of her emotions into bright, sunny thoughts. She loved this child. Couldn't believe she'd actually given birth to this lovely and lively creation. Tess felt truly blessed.

Erin's room would have been the dream of any little girl. The four-poster bed with its frilly pink canopy. The white dresser, bookcase and desk, all matching. The pink curtains that matched the canopy and the bedspread. Even the carpet was pink. The whole room was feminine. Almost too much so. It simply didn't seem to fit her daughter's character, what with Erin's love of cars and sports, and her abhorrence of dresses, or anything dainty or lacy, for that matter.

On her first visit into her daughter's room, Tess had found out that this furniture, the bedspread and curtains, had been a gift for Erin on her eighth birthday.

A gift from her grandmother. Helen Minster. Erin had been excited about the prospect of having her room redecorated. But then, without even asking Erin, Helen had all this white furniture delivered. Erin hated her room. She'd wanted bunk beds, not a stupid, frilly canopy. But Dylan had scolded her and told her that she shouldn't be ungrateful. He didn't want her to hurt her grandmother's feelings. So the furniture stayed.

"Here it is," Erin said.

The mask was large. A full-size replica of Tutankhamen's death mask. The plaster had been painstakingly hand-molded. It was by no means perfect, but the Egyptian face was certainly discernible. The plaster had been spray-painted with gold paint, and Erin was in the process of adding deep blue paint that obviously represented the lapis on the real mask.

"It's beautiful," Tess said. "You and Toby are doing a great job."

"Toby's coming tomorrow so we can finish it," Erin told her. "It's due on Monday."

Then Erin launched into a long story explaining why Toby couldn't come today. That his grandmother was in a nursing home and he had to drive a kabillion miles to visit her.

The room grew quiet suddenly, and Tess glanced at her daughter. Erin was fidgeting with the end of her belt, the tiny tail dangling from the buckle. Something was obviously on the child's mind, and Tess thought she knew what was about to happen.

Up until this moment, all her time with Erin had been spent talking about Erin; her thoughts and feelings about school, her friends and teachers, her favorite things to do, to see, to wear, to eat. Tess had spent days learning everything there was to know about her daughter. And she'd loved every minute of it.

Tess had been content to let the child ramble from one subject to the next in her jubilant attempt to cram as much information as she could into their talks. But Tess knew Erin must be curious about her. The only information the child had gleaned was that Tess lived in Connecticut and was a doctor. Erin must want to know what her mother has been doing all these years, and why she hasn't been in Pine Meadow.

Those were questions she read in Erin's shadowed gaze—questions Tess wasn't afraid of answering.

Chapter Eight

"How long will you be staying?"

Erin's voice was so tentative and shy, it ripped at Tess's heart.

"Today?" Tess asked. "Why, I'll stay as long as you like, sweetheart."

"No, I mean…" Again, the child's tone was timid. "I mean in town. How long will you be staying in Pine Meadow?"

"Oh, honey," Tess said, wrapping her arm lovingly around Erin's shoulder. "I don't want you to worry. Everything's going to work out fine. I won't let us lose touch again."

One corner of Erin's mouth tipped up endearingly. "I like that."

Tess's brows raised in inquiry.

The child's eyes averted shyly. "I like it when you call me those names. You know, sweetheart and honey."

Squeezing her tight, Tess said, "Well, you are my sweetheart. And my honey."

Erin giggled, hugging her mom around the waist, burying her face in Tess's stomach. Tess went all warm and quivery inside, and the love she felt seemed to expand and grow, as if her heart was a big balloon filling with more and more fuzzy emotion. The feeling was so intense it almost hurt, but it was the nicest kind of pain.

The edge of the mattress compressed as Tess sat down.

"I don't really know how long I'm staying," she continued quietly, honestly.

The idea of leaving Erin behind while she went back up north to continue in her new medical practice was upsetting to Tess. She hadn't really thought about it until this very moment.

"But you can bet," she said, "I won't leave without saying goodbye, or giving you my telephone number and address. I imagine you'll be visiting me up in Connecticut if your dad says it's okay."

"Ya mean it?" Erin's eyes lit up.

Tess nodded, chuckling. "I mean it. If your dad agrees."

"Oh, he'll let me come," the child said. "If he says no I'll just pitch a hissy fit until he gives in." Then her voice took on a low, conspiratorial tone. "That's how I get my way."

The smile on Tess's mouth faded. She couldn't believe what she was hearing. Granted, she hadn't knowingly been a parent for very long, but logic alone dictated that Erin needed to be called down for her manipulative manner. A scheming attitude simply wasn't fitting behavior for the child.

Yes, her daughter's love and respect were important to her, and Tess wanted those things desperately. But Tess wasn't Erin's friend. She wasn't someone to whom Erin should be confessing this kind of thing.

"Erin, your father loves you. Very much." Tess tried to keep the mild irritation she felt from her voice. "He only does what he thinks is best for you. If he feels you shouldn't come to Connecticut, then…you won't—"

"B-but," Erin said, her shoulders rounding, her hands lifting palm up in vehement objection, "I want to see you."

"I know you do." Tess spoke calmly, with a great deal of assurance. "And I want to see you. If you can't come visit me, then I'll come visit you."

The child looked a little less panicked. But Tess also knew a lesson had been learned here. She'd drawn a line. Erin knew there were boundaries she couldn't cross with her mother. That Tess had every intention of siding with Dylan in parental decisions. And also that Erin would not be allowed to play one of her parents against the other. Tess supposed there would be many instances like this in the future. She could only hope she'd clearly identify and then follow through in the handling of all of them as adeptly as she had this one.

Erin tinkered with the paintbrushes that sat on her desk, sulking. But it was evident that she had more she wanted to discuss. Tess remained quiet and waited with patience.

Without looking up, the child finally asked, "How come you waited so long to come see me?"

"Come here, hon," Tess coaxed softly. "Come sit next to me and I'll tell you all about it."

And there, in the close confines of the bedroom, Tess did just that. She told her daughter the truth, or rather, specific highlights of the truth. This child needed to know that her mother hadn't abandoned her. That her mother would have moved heaven and earth to have been with her…if she'd only been given the chance.

Soon, the two of them were stretched out on the bed. Erin, asking questions, Tess, answering them as best she could.

"But if you didn't know I was alive," Erin said, "how did you find out about me?"

"I didn't know a thing about you until I saw you at your dad's garage that first day."

"Oh." Erin reached up and rubbed an itch on her nose. "So that's why you took off so fast."

Tess nodded. "I was…shocked."

"What made you come back to Pine Meadow at all?"

"I, ah…" Tess hesitated, deciding not to bring up the bank account she'd found until she had more information. "I found some paperwork among my father's things that I needed to check on. Paperwork that led me here. So I drove down. And then I met you."

It was an awfully simplistic explanation of the facts, and Tess hoped it would suffice.

"So you really did love my dad when you guys were young?"

"Honey, I loved your dad more than words can describe." Tess smiled. "He was a rebel. A bad boy. And I fell for him so hard, and so completely, it's scary to me even now."

Erin giggled. "If you were to talk to my grandmother, she'd say he's still a rebel. But I like that about him. He doesn't let anybody tell him what to do.''

''I like that about him, too.'' The spontaneous comment slipped from Tess's lips.

''Grandmother harps on Dad all the time,'' Erin said, sudden sadness tingeing her tone. ''About everything. Sometimes I just don't understand her.''

Tess only listened. She didn't want to talk about Helen Minster.

Just then a knock on the door had them both twisting to look across the room. Dylan stood in the open doorway, and Tess's heart skipped a crazy beat. How long had he been standing there? she wondered. How much of her story had he overheard?

''Hamburgers are on,'' he said. ''If you ladies wouldn't mind, I could use some help carrying the rest of the food out to the picnic table.''

''Sure, Dad.'' Erin bounded off the bed and out the door like a bouncing ball.

Tess's smile was unsure, self-conscious as she stood. ''Our daughter sure is energetic.''

Dylan's chuckle was a sexy rumble deep in his throat.

''Like a nuclear reactor,'' he said.

She left the room feeling shaky, and knew that it had nothing to do with the heart-to-heart talk she'd just had with Erin, and everything to do with being in close proximity to the man who had fathered her child.

In the middle of the following week, Tess was in her hotel room, putting a light coat of mascara on her lashes. She'd become caught in a decadent rut of sleeping late, then going for a long invigorating walk, enjoying a little brunch and then taking a nice long soak in the tub.

What with college, and then med school and then completing her difficult residency, Tess had *never* had the luxury of simply being lazy, so she was loving this pampering she was able to give herself now. Her days were pretty much her own and she had no reason to hurry to do anything as her first appointment of each day was meeting her daughter's bus a little after three in the afternoon.

Every day, Tess felt she and Erin were growing closer, and she loved every single minute she spent with her daughter. Of course, spending every afternoon with Erin meant seeing Dylan every day, too. And even though Tess's meetings with him were minimal, the air sparked and crackled like fireworks on the fourth of July.

The attraction they felt was stronger than ever. And worse, they hadn't had a chance to talk. As they both knew they should.

Well, to be completely honest, it wasn't that they hadn't had a chance to talk. It was more they simply…hadn't.

Yes, they were both adults. Yes, they knew they needed to talk out what had happened between them in Paradise. Yes, they needed to come to some kind of agreement as to how to handle their unruly feelings. But they were also very good at avoiding the issue, she decided as she tightly screwed the cap on her tube of mascara.

Not that avoidance was easy; the fact that they hadn't discussed things made itself known in silent screams every single time they were together. But evasion *was* easier than actually facing the gargantuan subject of what they were feeling for each other.

The knock on her hotel room door startled her to the point that she dropped the mascara into the sink. Who could that be? Housekeeping knew her routine by now. The maid knew not to come clean the room until after she'd left at three. Giving the digital clock a quick glance, she saw that it was only two-fifteen.

Dylan? Had he finally come to confront her? To force her into talking about—

Again, the silence was interrupted by a knock. Steeling herself, she crossed the small room and opened the door. But nothing would have prepared her for what awaited on the other side.

"M-M-Mrs. Minster."

The elderly woman's appearance at her door so shocked Tess that her eyes went wide and she felt paralyzed. But immediately following her knee-jerk reaction, she made an attempt to recover, furious at herself for a dim-witted, stuttering greeting.

"Tess" was all the woman said.

Helen Minster's hair was streaked with gray, but was cut and coiffed to perfection. The deep green of her dress was just the right shade to set off her hazel eyes. The black leather handbag she carried matched the pumps on her feet. She looked calm, cool and utterly professional. But Tess wouldn't have expected Dylan's mother to look anything else. Then Tess noticed something else. The woman also carried a manila file.

Silent seconds ticked by. The woman's chin tipped up. Just a tiny fraction. But the immediate result was that Tess was left feeling looked down upon. Damn!

How was it that Helen Minster, with a single look, could make her feel like a worthless child again?

Doing her best to salvage some self-control, Tess said, "You look like you have something on your mind. Would you like to come in?"

Ignoring Tess's comment and her question, Helen entered the room. And Tess shut the door.

Self-consciousness flared inside her like a beacon when Tess turned and saw the unmade bed, the damp towel that had been tossed over the desk chair.

She snatched up the towel, tossed it into the bathroom and shut the door. "Housekeeping hasn't been in today."

Again, Helen ignored her.

"Please sit down," Tess said, offering her the one plush chair in the small room. And she was actually surprised when Dylan's mother accepted with a murmured thank-you. Tess turned the desk chair around and sat down.

Then she waited.

During the stiff silence that followed, Tess conjured all manner of things Helen Minster might say to her.

"How dare you come back to Pine Meadow after all this time?"

"I want you packed and gone in twenty-four hours!"

"You stay away from my son and my granddaughter."

"Do you really want Erin to find out what you are? What you came from?"

The possibilities made Tess's insides quiver as she contemplated how she should respond to Helen's mean questions, her angry demands and sharp accusations.

''So—''

Tess actually started at the woman's first word, but thank goodness Mrs. Minster had her gaze fastened on the purse she clutched tightly in her lap, the folder resting neatly underneath.

''—you came about the account.''

It was as though Tess had received a swift kick to her diaphragm. She couldn't breathe, let alone speak.

Silence settled again. Deafening. Claustrophobic.

''Well?''

Helen's hawkish eyes were on Tess now, making her feel like prey.

''The money is the reason you've come back to Pine Meadow?''

There was a strong sense of ownership in her tone when she spoke the name of the town. Hoarding and protective, at the same time. Tess heard it and took it to heart.

Mustering her tattered wits, Tess answered, ''Yes.'' She cleared her throat, hoping to strengthen her voice. ''That's exactly why I've come.''

Helen squared her shoulders and sat up straighter, if that was possible.

''I refused to believe that was you in the bank last week,'' the woman said. ''I just couldn't accept the idea of having to deal with this...distasteful mess. Again.''

Just which *distasteful mess* Mrs. Minster was talking about, Tess wasn't certain. Was she referring to her own loathsome behavior where the money was concerned? Or was she talking about Tess and her teen pregnancy?

Tess thought it was a pretty easy guess.

"I'd put the entire matter out of my head," Helen went on. "Hadn't thought about it in years, actually."

"You hadn't thought about it?" Tess wasn't sure which stunned her more, Helen's almost breezy avowal—a declaration, by the way, that made Tess feel completely valueless—or the challenge she heard in her own words. Embers of anger glowed deep in the pit of her belly. "How could you *not* think about it? How could you not think about me, and my father, and what happened all those years ago, when Erin is here? Surely you see her. Surely you—"

"Of course I see her." Helen cut her off smoothly. "I see my granddaughter quite often, in fact. Someone has to see that she's being raised properly." Then she softly added, "Although Dylan makes my efforts so difficult." Her head tilted slightly. "But, you see, I don't associate Erin with…" Her sentence went unfinished as she vaguely waved her hand in a single, short swipe, her face contorting a bit, as if she'd bitten into a thin slice of lemon.

That distasteful mess. Tess almost heard the awful description repeated aloud. And the anger inside her flared. Trying hard to contain her emotions, she decided that it would be in her own best interest to keep her head, not to allow her strong, roiling feelings to rule her tongue. At least, not until *after* she discovered the information she was looking for about the bank account book she'd found among her father's things.

"Anyway—"

Helen smoothed an imagined wrinkle from the immaculate fabric of her dress and Tess got the distinct message that the woman didn't intend to talk about the offensive situation that happened to take place ten years earlier.

"—as I said, I couldn't believe you'd come back to Pine Meadow. I thought my eyes must be playing tricks on me." Mrs. Minster daintily moistened her lipstick-coated lips. "However, I couldn't put the notion aside any longer after this morning."

Tess raised her brows a curious fraction.

"I had a general meeting with the bank staff," she told Tess. "Afterward I was approached by Pete Taylor. He's an employee at the bank. But then you know that, since you talked with him last week. He told me you'd been in to see him."

Folding her hands in her lap, Tess thought it best to simply remain silent for the moment.

"By the way," Helen said, "I'm sorry to hear about your father."

Cold. The woman was cold. Sorry was the last thing she was feeling. That was clear. Tess realized that Helen Minster only offered the condolence because that's what propriety dictated. There was certainly no sympathy or comfort in the offer.

Tess couldn't help but feel sorry for Dylan that he'd had to grow up with such a woman as his mother.

"If you'll fill out the paperwork that Pete provided for you," Helen said, rushing into the business at hand, "I can see that the account is turned over to you today. And you can be on your way back to... wherever it is you've been these past ten years."

As she spoke, she picked up, and then opened, the file she brought with her. She handed Tess some papers, and Tess reached out and took them.

Listed on the crisp white paper was a printout of her father's account; the date of the initial deposit, as well as the dates and amounts of the accruing interest. Tess stared down at the sheets. Finally she rubbed the fingers of her free hand back and forth across her fore-head. Then she gazed up at Mrs. Minster and shook her head.

"You do want the money, don't you?" she asked Tess. "It was your father's. Now it's yours."

For a moment, Tess didn't trust herself to speak. What did this woman think? That she could stuff some money into Tess's hand, pat her on the head and scoot her out of town? Helen Minster's audacity was infuriating.

Calm down. The silent advice made Tess pause. *Hold back that anger for a few minutes more.*

She fortified herself with a deep inhalation, and quietly asked, "Where did the money come from, Mrs. Minster?"

The woman's gaze went flat. "How am I supposed to know that? It was your father's life savings, maybe?" She shrugged. "It isn't my business to ask where my customers get their money. It's only my business to carefully protect that money. And that's exactly what I've done. Now what I'd suggest you do is—"

"Just stop it!" Tess barely suppressed the overwhelming urge to fling the papers right in Helen's face. But instead, she crushed them in one fist as she jumped from the chair and paced the length of the small hotel room. "You *know* this money came from you. You and your husband. You deposited this money in my father's name to ease your conscience."

Helen's lips pursed. "I guess I should have expected you to say something so...*ugly.*"

"It's the truth," Tess spit out. "And I do agree. It's ugly as hell." She gritted her teeth. "But you want to know what's even uglier?"

She watched Helen grow utterly still, her eyes narrowing warily.

Her tone was low and ruthless as she said, "What that money bought."

"Don't," Helen said, her voice a raspy whisper.

But Tess barreled ahead, the flames of her anger burning bright. "That money bought a child. *My* child," she said, viciously jabbing at her chest with her index finger. "That money bought my happiness. That money bought all the years I missed with my daughter. I didn't get to see her take her first step. Say her first word. I didn't get to hear her recite the alphabet. Or get on the school bus for the first time. I missed it all! I missed everything."

She swiped at a lock of hair that had fallen into her face. "Everything," she continued, "except the grief." Tess felt tears well in her eyes. "I spent years grieving for a baby that I was told was born dead. And all I have to show for that is a lump sum of cash that's sitting in Minster Savings and Loan." The harsh bark of laughter erupted painfully around the huge knot of sorrow in her throat. "Granted, it is a lot of money. Boy, this cost you plenty, didn't it? I remember the doctor that delivered my baby. You must have paid him a great deal to lie like he did. And the nurse. She, too, must have cost you. How much did you pay them, Helen?"

Her use of the woman's first name was meant to reveal the tremendous disrespect Tess felt for Dylan's mother at this moment, and blinding fury was the motivating factor. That, combined with the huge sense of being wronged.

Helen Minster's chest rose and fell, rapidly, the only sign that she was feeling any emotion at all.

"I paid them a lot." She kept perfect control of herself. "A whole lot."

Their gazes locked tight.

"So," Tess said, "you admit it. You admit to *buying* my child. *Robbing* me of raising my own baby."

The older woman winced. What? Tess wondered. Was she actually causing fissures in that façade of granite Helen was wearing?

"I only did what I thought was best for my boy," she said.

"He was a man," Tess said pointedly. "A twenty-year-old man."

"He was a *child*. A naïve boy who knew nothing. Nothing about life. Nothing about goals. And he was about to throw away everything."

A thin sheen of perspiration glistened on Helen's upper lip. "But then," she added as a quiet aside, "he's always been bent on throwing away everything."

The woman's complicated statement held hidden messages that evidently dealt with the present, but Tess was too involved with what happened in the past to give it too much thought.

"If you think Dylan becoming a father meant he was ruining his life," Tess said, "then why didn't you just leave me and my baby alone. Why didn't you just let me raise my daughter?"

"You? Raise a Minster?"

Tess wasn't hurt by Helen's questions, she was simply amazed that the woman asked them in such a natural, matter-of-fact manner.

"You had nothing," Helen continued. "You had no prospects of ever having anything. No breeding, no background, no education."

Pride surged up within her. "Well, I have an education now. In fact, I'm practicing medicine. I'm a full-fledged medical doctor."

Her attempt to impress Dylan's mother fell flat as it became apparent that the declaration didn't affect the woman in the least. And the effort left Tess feeling hollow and more than a little angry at herself for having tried.

Helen's only response was, "Ten years ago, you had nothing."

Tucking her bottom lip firmly between her teeth, Tess remained silent. She couldn't argue with the truth.

"Tess," Helen began. Then she paused, inhaled deeply and squared her shoulders. "I don't expect you to understand the reasons behind what my husband and I did all those years ago."

Her voice was barely a whisper as Tess said, "Don't forget to include my father on your list of culprits."

"Your father..." Helen Minster shook her head. "Your father did exactly what we told him to do. We talked him into believing that sending Erin to us was the right thing to do. For you. For Dylan. For everyone concerned. And he believed us because we were right."

She unlatched her purse and pulled out a tissue. "You and your father couldn't offer Erin anything. While my husband and I...we had everything to offer the child."

Tess's spine straightened as a thought struck her with force. "You planned to raise Erin yourself."

"I did. I planned to bring her up as a proper young lady." Helen went quiet, then said, "But you know what they say about the best laid plans."

Humorless irony tugged at one corner of Tess's mouth. "I guess that means Dylan had other plans."

"Didn't he always?" Daintily Helen dabbed her chin with the tissue. "We hadn't had that child under our roof for eighteen months and Dylan up and proclaimed he couldn't work in the bank. He reneged on his promise to join the family business. That boy's stubbornness killed his father. And then he moved out of Minster House. He took that child off to a tiny little apartment. Even after all I tried to do for him. Even after all the money I doled out. He still managed to ruin his life. His life, and Erin's."

Confusion knit Tess's brow. "But I don't see how he's ruined his life. He's doing what he wants. His auto shop seems successful enough."

"Please." Helen sniffed. "Dylan struggles from month to month."

"He has money problems?"

"He hasn't come to me for money yet," Helen said. "But he will, you mark my words. And he isn't able to give Erin the things she needs."

Tess thought about her cheerful, contented daughter, remembering her easy laughter, her quick wit. "Erin seems happy enough to me. I think Dylan's doing a great job—"

"That child is a mess," Helen interrupted. "She's always got some tool or other in her hands. And she's always covered from head to toe in axle grease. It's horrible."

Remembering how Erin's eyes lit up when she told Tess about the car she built with her father, Tess decided her daughter was a normal, boisterous ten-year-old, grease or no grease. Erin and Dylan were doing what they loved to do. And they were having fun and spending lots of time together doing it, too. Time that would bond their father/daughter relationship forever. Their lives seemed healthy. And very happy. But arguing that point with Helen Minster would be futile.

After a moment, Helen said, ''I never in my life thought I'd find myself in this position.''

A frown planted itself in Tess's forehead. She couldn't fathom what the woman meant.

''I never imagined,'' she continued, ''that I'd have to ask for your discretion.''

''My...?'' Tess shook her head, having no clue where the conversation was going.

''Tess, Dylan and I don't have the best of relationships.'' Helen paused long enough to pat the tissue against her upper lip. ''We didn't ten years ago, and we still don't today. But I love my son. Just like any mother loves her child. And I don't know what it would do to our relationship if he were ever to find out about...the money I paid your father.''

Her breath left her in a whoosh. ''Dylan doesn't know.'' Feelings flooded through her, a powerful mixture of relief and elation. He hadn't been aware of the conspiracy to steal her child from her. The revelation was overwhelming. And for a long moment she let herself bask in it.

Suddenly, she was aware that Helen had grown still and quiet, pensive as she waited for Tess to give some response.

''You're asking me to keep the bank account a secret,'' Tess said. ''You don't want me to tell Dylan.''

''That's exactly what I'm asking.''

Tess thought a moment, then asked, ''Why? Why would you think I'd do something like that for you? After what you did to me.''

"You won't be doing it for me," Helen said softly. "You'll be doing it for Dylan."

That took the wind out of Tess's sails.

"You used to have deep feelings for my son..."

A shiver raced up Tess's spine as she pondered those potent feelings, and how they had returned, full-force, since she'd come back to Pine Meadow.

"I'm asking you to think about him," she went on. "Think about what's best for Dylan. He'd be hurt if he knew. Our relationship is tenuous at best. If he found out about this, it would destroy what little we do have."

Tess looked at this woman, thoughts ricocheting in her brain like so many Ping-Pong balls. Helen was pushing Tess into silence. Silence that would save Dylan from being hurt. Silence that would save Helen from being hurt. Well...

"What about me?" she blurted. "What about the pain I felt when I was told my baby died? What about the grief I suffered? The long years of grief?"

Helen sighed. "I can't do anything about that. Tess, I can't give you an apology for something I'm not sorry about."

Lowering her gaze a couple of feet, Tess noticed that Helen had begun to twist the tissue in her fingers.

"I am sorry your father didn't transfer the money to another bank," she continued. "I am sorry he didn't spend it. That he didn't burn the bankbook along with all the statements. But I can't apologize for doing what I thought was best for everyone concerned. For you and Dylan. And especially for Erin."

Chapter Nine

In the end, Tess agreed to keep silent about the money Dylan's parents deposited in the account to her father as payment for Erin. Tess wanted badly to believe she hadn't agreed to be a party in this plot—and plot was exactly how she thought of it, a plot to keep Dylan in the dark—for Helen Minster.

Dylan's mother was a cold and calculating woman. She was someone Tess had, for as long as she could remember, feared. Someone who had made her feel unworthy.

Tess had thought that when she'd returned to Pine Meadow, all grown up with doctorate in hand and success in her future, that she'd no longer feel inferior. She'd been wrong. Helen Minster would never look at Tess as an equal. Never.

What amazed Tess the most was that Dylan's mother had been the one who had acted in such a despicable manner, yet the woman could still look down her nose at others.

So why had Tess agreed to keep the money a secret from Dylan?

There were several reasons. Erin had been her number one motivation. Tess didn't even want to begin to imagine how devastating it would be for her daughter to find out what Helen had done. How the child's own grandmother had completely severed any chance Erin had of being raised by her own mother.

Then there was Dylan. Helen had tweaked something inside Tess when she'd played on Tess's past feelings for Dylan. There had been a time when Tess had loved the man with all of her heart, with every ounce of her soul. He, too, would be devastated to discover his mother's wicked deception. In honor of what they had once shared—not to mention the overwhelming emotions he stirred in her since her return to town—Tess thought it best to keep the news from him.

And then there had been the part Tess's father had played in the whole horrible scheme. Yes, Tess continued to feel utterly disappointed in her dad for allowing himself to be caught up in the manipulative plot. But he'd given her all he could over the years—even though he'd taken away so very much. Tess sighed sadly when she thought of all he'd denied her. However, she still loved him. How could she not? He was her father. He was family. He'd taken care of her. Loved her. Sacrificed for her. Out of respect for his memory, Tess decided to keep his one indiscretion a secret.

"Happy Birthday!"

Erin's friends began to sing the Birthday Song as the waitress of the pizza parlor brought to the table the cake with its ten flaming candles. Tess gazed at her grinning daughter and joined in the singing.

A heated, poignant rush of emotion washed over her—emotion Tess had discovered was pure maternal love. There was nothing like it, nothing to compare to the intense feelings a mother felt toward her child. She was truly blessed to be here at Erin's tenth birthday party. Truly blessed to know her daughter. Truly blessed to have the chance to hug her, love her, the chance to mold and guide the woman Erin would become.

Tess realized suddenly that if she hadn't come across that tainted bank account, she might never have discovered she even had a daughter. The idea left Tess feeling a twinge of bleakness at the prospect, then all the more content that circumstances had turned out as they had.

Once the last notes of the song faded, Dylan called out, "Don't forget to make a wish before you blow out those candles, Erin."

A smile glittered in his vivid green gaze, and Tess's heart *ka-chunked* in her chest. Almost a week had passed since she'd conspired with Helen, and every single time she was with Dylan she was bothered by the acute awareness that she was lying to him.

Yes, she knew that keeping the secret was saving him from being hurt, but she still felt guilt-ridden. And that guilt was compounded mightily by the allure they battled daily.

She wanted Dylan so badly she could almost taste the sweet desire that pulsed through her veins. He wanted her, too. That was clear to her every moment they were together. The longing in the looks he gave her couldn't be hidden, even if he'd tried, which he didn't. And there were times Tess was certain that, if Erin were to leave them alone for even a single second, he'd reach out for her, touch her in a way that would make her writhe with pleasure. But, luckily, they hadn't had the occasion to be alone.

Tess sighed, admitting that luck had very little to do with it. She'd made sure they hadn't had a chance to be alone. Because she was frightened witless of being alone with him now that she knew he was completely innocent of wrongdoing. She was so confused by her feelings. By the intensity of the emotions that grew, day by day.

Knowing he was blameless should have freed her, should have erased every bit of the doubt she felt about acting upon her physical attraction, her overwhelming need.

But the thing holding her at bay was the guilt. The guilt she felt over keeping the secret. Guilt that constantly poked and prodded at her conscience.

As Erin busied herself opening brightly colored packages, her friends chattering in delight, Tess felt Dylan's eyes drawing her attention. Sure enough, he was staring at her. In a manner that made his sensuous thoughts quite clear. In a manner that made her feel as if they were the only two people alive on earth. Her cheeks flamed with heat. Slowly he got up from the table and came to stand beside her, never once taking his eyes off her face.

"I need you." His whisper was for her ears alone.

Her eyes widened, a delicious shiver shimmying across her skin.

He quickly added, "I need to talk to you."

For an instant, Tess wondered if he was amending his statement, but after one look at his handsome face, she was certain she hadn't misheard his original words—or his intent. The need clouding his gaze was absolute proof that her ears hadn't failed her.

"I can't stand this any longer," he told her.

The need evinced in his voice made her pulse go haywire, her blood pressure skyrocket.

"We have to talk."

She understood. She, too, had suffered the profound tension that throbbed and pulsed, seeming to have a life of its own.

Reaching up, she crossed her arms, smoothed her hands up and down her biceps and acquiesced with a small nod.

"You'll follow me back to my house?" he asked softly.

Again she nodded.

"Erin's asked to go to Wendy's sleepover," he said. "We'll have the house to ourselves."

That news scared Tess witless. And excited her beyond belief.

He turned back to the party taking place in the pizza parlor, a "friends only" affair that Erin had requested. The child had told Tess that she didn't relish the "family" party she'd have to endure later this week. A stuffy party with no children her own age, only aunts and uncles…and her grandmother.

Tess was happy that Dylan had agreed to such a gathering as this one with its gooey pizza, sodas, ice cream and cake, and a hoard of squealing friends. Oh, and presents. Lots of presents. Tess was also delighted to be a part of Erin's special day, the first birthday she'd ever celebrated with her daughter. But Tess really disliked the fact that her merriment was hampered by worry over her impending "talk" with Dylan.

* * *

The moon hung fat in the sky, so close to the earth that Tess could easily see the craters with their gray-blue valleys against the stark whiteness of the orb. The night was lit up so bright that few stars could be seen twinkling in the heavens.

As she'd promised, Tess had followed Dylan back to his house. Erin had gathered together her pajamas, her slippers and her toothbrush, and then Dylan and Tess had taken their daughter to Wendy's house. April and Wendy bounded out the front door and the girls had giggled themselves silly right there in the front yard. The one thing Tess would never forget, however, was that, before she and Dylan could drive off, Erin had rushed back to the car at the last moment and planted a sweet kiss on Tess's cheek.

"Bye," Erin had whispered. "I will see ya tomorrow."

The question in her daughter's soft brown eyes practically split Tess's heart in two. "Of course, you will," she'd assured Erin softly. Erin had then gone around to the driver's side of the car and had given her dad a good-night kiss.

The ride back to Dylan's had been made in silence. And Tess was relieved to have a few minutes to ponder again this wondrous thing called motherhood. The heart-wrenching emotions Tess experienced when she was with Erin were all so new to her. Overwhelming in their proportions, she sometimes thought her heart simply could not hold everything she felt for the beautiful child she had given birth to. Tess wondered if the magnitude of her feelings would…wear off. Would the poignancy, the deep richness of the emotions she felt wane with the passing of time? Was the overpow-

ering nature of her feelings due to the fact that she'd
missed the first ten years of her daughter's life?

As soon as they had arrived at Dylan's home, he'd
ushered her out back and then he went inside to heat
up some cider. When he returned and handed her a
steaming mug, she was still contemplating the same
issue.

"When Erin kissed me," she said quietly, settling
the bottom of the mug against one palm, "my heart
filled with so much love, I thought it would burst."

Dylan eased himself down beside her on the
wooden bench, one corner of his mouth hitching up.

"I wonder..." She paused, a sudden sense of shyness creeping up on her. "I wonder if women who
have been with their children from the very beginning
continue to feel this awesome, breathtaking—" she
shook her head as words escaped her "—emotion?"

His mouth pulled into a full-fledged smile.

"I can't speak for moms," he told her. "But as
Erin's dad, I can say that every time that child hugs
me, or kisses my cheek, or even when she graces me
with a simple smile, she just takes away my breath.
She always has." His tone lowered as he added, "I
expect she always will."

Tess swallowed a sip of the cider, the taste of apple
and cinnamon sweet on her tongue. She lowered the
mug, and studied Dylan's handsome face. He was such
a good and loving father. A pure-hearted and decent
person. And in that moment—that very instant—she
was struck with a stupefying revelation.

She loved this man. Had never stopped loving him
in all the years they had spent apart.

What she had taken for mere physical attraction was
a thin veil that disguised the deep and powerful love

that churned within her, that had lain dormant for so very long.

There were reasons why she shouldn't. Plenty of reasons.

He'd hurt her all those years ago. With his rejection. With his angry accusations and name-calling. He'd caused her pain and sorrow, humiliation and anguish. Such pain she'd been sure, at times, she simply wouldn't survive it.

But she had.

Now here she sat, ten years later, facing the man in whom she had placed all her hopes, all her dreams. The man she had loved—*still loved*—with every fiber of her being. Every ounce of her soul.

And he sat beside her, looking at her with unmistakable, unadulterated desire shining in his green eyes.

Dylan leaned over and took the mug from her hands. Then he set them both on the ground. When he straightened, he slid closer to her until their knees and thighs were pressed together, and the heat of his body seeped into her skin.

"I love Erin," he said. "And your coming to Pine Meadow has been good for her. I'm happy about that. I'm happy that you've become important to her. A necessary part of her life. I'd been worried that she wasn't getting the feminine influence she needed. Now, I know you're going to take care of that. Your being a part of our daughter's life only means good things for Erin. Even though, I realize, there's still plenty of things you and I need to work out. But..."

His face pinched up, as if he was feeling a discomfiting emotion.

"But I don't want to talk about Erin tonight," he

admitted softly. "I want to talk about us. You and me. And this...*thing* we're feeling."

Tess was consumed by the intensity emanating off him, but she was also vaguely aware that he'd slid his hand across the back of the seat, that he'd inadvertently begun to toy with a small lock of her hair, almost as if he couldn't keep his hands to himself.

She knew exactly how he felt. She ached to touch him, to run her hands over his chest, to at least take his hand in hers, entwine her fingers with his. But not knowing whether he felt good or bad about this undeniable *thing* between them, she held the urges at bay. He might want her, but he might not *want* to want her. Before she acted on her own impulses, she had to know how he felt about his.

He smoothed his index finger along the outer curve of her ear, slowly, sensually. And his gaze darkened.

"I want so badly to kiss you," he said. "To hold you against me. But I just can't. I can't allow myself the pleasure."

A heavy sigh escaped him. A sigh that conveyed all the effort it was taking to keep himself from giving in to temptation—temptation *she* was causing. A tiny thrill shot through her.

"Not until we talk." His gaze roamed over her face, lingering on her mouth. "Not until I tell you what's on my mind. Not until I—" he looked her in the eyes "—apologize."

"Dylan..."

He pressed his fingertips gently against her lips. "Shh," he crooned. "Let me finish. This has bothered me for—" his exhalation was rueful "—*ever*. Ever since I said those horrible things to you all those years ago."

His fingertips trailed from her mouth to her jaw. "A simple 'I'm sorry,'" he continued, "just isn't enough. I need to explain. To try to make you understand what I was going through back then."

Tess didn't want to remember those awful moments, but in an instant, she was back there. In that frightful place. That frightful time. At the vulnerable age of seventeen.

The angry look on Dylan's face had been enough to bring her to tears. But the hostile words he'd flung at her had been like deadly arrows he'd aimed straight at her heart, and he couldn't have been more successful in killing her spirit, even if he had wielded an actual weapon.

"How could you have let this happen?" he'd shouted at her just after she'd tearfully revealed her pregnancy to him.

Tess didn't remember the exact sequence of his mean and furious accusations. All she remembered was the pain she felt as he pelted her with each one.

"You're trying to trap me. You don't want me to succeed. And you're not interested in making anything of yourself, either. You'd be happy to be stuck for the rest of your life in a dingy little one-room apartment. With half a dozen hungry mouths to feed. My parents were right about you."

He had spit out other slurs against her. Insulting and slanderous. Hurtful beyond belief. But the one that wounded her the most, the one she would never forget, was when he'd agreed with his parents' opinion of her.

The Minsters—Dylan included—would always think of her as the girl from the wrong side of town.

Tess had stood there silently and had taken everything Dylan had doled out. She'd absorbed his anger.

Submitted to his wrath. Because she had felt she deserved it. She'd felt to blame. She'd gotten pregnant. In her innocent mind, she decided he was justified in dealing her any punishment he saw fit. And punish her, he had. With irrefutable rejection.

"I don't want to have anything more to do with you."

His parting words rang in her head, like the reverberating ring of a death knell. She blinked, a single, silent tear slipping down her face, its momentum tickling her skin, bringing her out of the nightmare of the past and back into the present.

"Ah, Tess." Dylan's voice was raw, and he gently swiped at the moist track on the side of her nose with the pad of his thumb. "The things I said still hurt you. Even after all this time."

His observation didn't require a reply. She couldn't very well deny the pain she felt, the pain she knew was evident on her face, in her tears. But there was something she felt she had to say, had wanted to say way back then and was never given the chance.

"I'm sorry I ruined everything for us," she said; her voice sounded bruised and raw. "I didn't mean to get pregnant—"

"*We* got pregnant, Tess," he interrupted. "That was something that happened when we were together." He shook his head. "And if anything, I'm the one who should shoulder most of the blame. I was the older one. I never should have enticed you to become...physically intimate. You were just a child, really." He gazed off. "The first time we had sex you were only sixteen." Again, he shook his head with regret. "The only excuse I have is that I was young. Immature. Hormones had me listening to the wrong part of my anatomy. And, Tess, like stupid kids everywhere, I thought I was invincible. I thought *we* were. I never thought in a million years something like that would happen to us.''

His intense gaze commanded her complete attention. ''I had no right to blame you,'' he said softly. ''But it was so damned easy. Easier than blaming myself. Which is what I *should* have done. I should have taken responsibility for my actions.'' His hand went slack on her shoulder for a moment, his voice dropping to a mere whisper as he added, ''Our lives would have turned out so differently if I had.''

Every instinct in her told her to be accepting and forgiving. But the years of pain she'd suffered through, the grief that had totally snuffed out her spirit, the blame she'd shouldered all these years, cried out for retribution...or at least some kind of acknowledgment.

''So,'' she found herself saying, ''why didn't you?''

He whispered her name on a groan. She heard the deep remorse he felt, and for a moment she was sorry she'd confronted him when he was already trying to apologize. However, even though she regretted her question, she didn't recant it. She'd suffered enough to deserve an answer.

''My life had been a wreck, a total disaster for about a month prior to...''

Dylan looked heavenward, evidently searching for a word or phrase to describe the event that initiated their terrible breakup.

''Your announcement,'' he said.

Tess remembered how he'd changed, remembered how hurt and confused she'd been by the distance he was slowly, but surely placing between them.

"You see," he continued, "my parents had found out about us. They started this campaign against you. Against our relationship. It was clear they wanted me to stop seeing you. They also began to actively lobby for change in other areas of my life. They threatened me, harassed me, pressured me, every day. Then they began lecturing me about my future. They told me it was time for me to get serious about my life. It was time to put away the toys, and by that they meant my motorcycle, my jeans, my leather jacket, my love of cars. They urged me, again and again, to find some respect for myself. To dress up in a business suit. To go work in the bank. They made this ready-made career they had in mind for me sound so...right."

For the life of her, Tess couldn't understand what was so new about that. The way she remembered it, from the very first time she and Dylan had talked, he'd complained about his parents' disapproval of his behavior. He'd always felt resentful that they couldn't accept him and love him for who he was. And he'd hated the idea of their trying to make him into something he wasn't.

"But," she said, "none of that was really unusual, was it? It's what they'd always done."

He nodded. "But something changed after they discovered our relationship. The lectures became more intense. They focused on the fact that you were so young. Too young to be influenced by me." He sighed. "And then there was the change in my dad. He started taking time to be with me. To show an interest in what I thought about things. I'd always believed my dad couldn't stand the sight of me. To have his attention...well, it was something I'd never had before. And every time Dad and I were together, my mother was so...happy.''

Dylan studied her a moment.

''They were my parents, Tess. I wanted them to be proud of me. I wanted to make them happy. Is that so wrong?''

She couldn't help but wonder just how many parents, her own father included, played on their children's desire to be loved and accepted to get them to toe the line. The thought saddened her, and she decided then and there that she would never force her own daughter to do or be anything other than what Erin wanted for herself.

''For the first time in my life,'' Dylan said, ''I seemed to have my parents' approval. And to keep it, I ended up promising to go to work in the bank.'' He paused a moment. ''I had no idea how I was going to tell you. I was so afraid I would lose your respect. I was still trying to find a way to explain, when you told me you were pregnant.''

He ran his fingers through his dark hair. ''The news was earth-shattering, to say the least. How was I ever going to explain to my father that I screwed up? Again.''

Tess noticed he no longer touched her. That he'd even backed away from her an inch or so, and she got the distinct impression that he felt he didn't deserve to be near her, to touch her, when he was revealing his motive behind rejecting her. And from the pained look on his handsome face, she knew the worst was yet to come.

''I just couldn't disappoint my dad,'' Dylan said. ''I just couldn't. So in a moment of weakness...a moment of pure panic, I turned on you. Completely. I blamed you for everything. It was so much easier to do that than to go home and face losing my father's respect altogether.''

Tilting her head to one side, Tess simply looked at him. She understood. She really did. She would have done anything to make her own father happy. He'd been all she had. And even though she now knew her father had taken part in keeping her from Erin all these years, Tess realized that didn't change how she felt about him. So she understood why Dylan had done what he had done, said what he had said. She was actually a little relieved because all this time she had believed his mean and spiteful words had been caused by something else. She'd thought all those years ago that Dylan had suspected she was pregnant even before she'd discovered the fact herself. That he'd become standoffish because he couldn't cope with the idea of becoming a father. She'd thought he'd rejected her because he didn't want her. Didn't want their child. To find out he'd turned away from her because of his parents actually softened the blow of what had happened to them.

One corner of his mouth curled in a sad smile. ''How does that old saying go? The one that says, 'You always hurt the one you love, the one you shouldn't hurt at all.' Well, that's how I've always felt about the way we parted. I hurt you. And I never should have. I'm terribly sorry. And I hope you'll forgive me.''

Tess reached out and took his hand in hers. ''You're forgiven.''

The smile he gave her made her feel warm and wonderful. She was glad to know the truth, to have the shadows of the past cleared up, and he seemed relieved to have had the chance to explain.

He rubbed his thumb over the hills and valleys of her knuckles. "It's so funny how fate works. As it turned out I ended up disappointing my parents anyway. I couldn't continue working at the bank...even though I tried. Hard. Especially after Erin came to us. Mom and Dad promised to help me raise Erin as long as I proceeded along on the right path. The path *they* chose for me. But I just couldn't. I hated being cooped up in that stuffy office, working with numbers all day. It just wasn't me." One of his shoulders hitched up a fraction. "So I quit."

Tess remained silent, feeling her only job here was to listen.

"Dad died shortly thereafter," he went on. "The doctor said it was a brain aneurysm, but my mother was sure he'd died because he was so worried, so upset. About me."

Dylan's stubbornness killed his father. Tess remembered Helen Minster's words. At the time Tess had thought it had simply been a figure of speech, a way for Dylan's mother to convey the depth of her husband's turmoil. However, now Tess was left wondering if Helen Minster really did believe what she'd said. If that was so, Tess thought it was a horrible burden Helen had placed on her son. An awful thought she'd put in Dylan's head.

"I took Erin away from Minster House," Dylan told her. "I needed to make a life for us. A life we could be happy with."

Tess eagerly pointed out, "It seems as though you've succeeded at that. Erin is happy. She's well-adjusted. She's intelligent. She's an all-around great kid. You've done a terrific job.''

His embarrassed grin charmed her to the tips of her toes.

After a moment he said, ''You know, when everything's said and done, we do have to admit that some good came out of your, ah, going away.''

Curiosity had her brows raising a fraction.

''If you'd have stayed here,'' he explained, ''you'd never have had the opportunity to go to college. You'd never have become a doctor.''

With no hesitation, Tess replied, ''I'd give it all up in a heartbeat...to have been able to be here to raise Erin.''

He slid his hand up to tenderly cup her cheek as he silently studied her gaze.

''But you have so much more to offer Erin now,'' he said, ''because of the hand fate dealt us.''

Tess pressed her palm to the back of his hand. ''It's important to me that you know our child means everything to me. That I want to be there for her. That I want only what's best for her.''

He whispered, ''I want to believe you.''

And then he covered her mouth with his.

His kiss short-circuited her thinking. All she did was *feel*. Warm, silky, sensuous sensations. His touch, his kiss, had always had the ability to leave her breathless, thoughtless, senseless. And this time was no exception.

Threading her fingers into his thick hair, she pulled him even closer. The scent of him, the taste of him, the feel of his body so close to hers, was enough to make her nearly wild with need.

His breath was erratic in her ear, his desire clearly

evident in his ardent kiss, and that only served to heat the passion in her blood even more.

"I want us to try again, Tess."

His words were a ragged whisper against her hot, moist mouth.

"I want us to have the chance that was taken away from us ten years ago."

Tiny bursts of joy exploded inside her, like dozens of miniature fireworks, colorful and glittering. The idea of spending the rest of her life with this man was overwhelming, to say the least. But a dark cloud hovered over the celebration going on in her head.

I want to believe you, his words echoed in her brain.

He hadn't said he believed her when she'd told him what Erin meant to her. He'd said he *wanted* to. There was a nuance of difference—a nuance that had a significant effect on her.

Doubt was inferred in his statement. About what? she couldn't help but wonder. Doubt about her feelings for Erin? Doubt about her future intentions? Tess didn't think so. She was sure the uncertainty he was obviously feeling hinged on the past. On *her* behavior in the past.

He's still holding on to the notion that I sent Erin back to him, she silently realized. *He still believes I lied to him about the circumstances surrounding Erin's birth.*

She wanted so badly to tell him her story again. To explain that she was innocent of any wrongdoing. That she was the one who had been wronged. By her own father. And by Dylan's parents.

However, it was with a sinking heart that she realized that the one piece to the puzzle that would exonerate her, prove her innocence beyond all doubt, was the secret she'd promised to keep from him.

Her whole body trembled. And although the tiny kisses he planted on her neck and jaw were utterly tantalizing, she knew the quaking inside her was caused by the helplessness she suddenly felt over this predicament.

"Wait," she murmured.

Tess didn't want him to have any doubts about her. "Dylan, stop."

He kissed her mouth again, and then raised up just enough to look into her face.

What could she say? her frantic mind wondered. How could she clear his doubts if she couldn't tell him the full truth?

She studied his gaze, vying for time.

"We need to slow down." The words slipped past her lips. "We can't rush this."

The chuckle vibrating in his chest was deep and sexy. "Oh," he said, "but I want to rush it. We've wasted too much time already."

"Lots of time *has* passed." She latched onto the excuse with both hands. "That's my point exactly. You've been through so much. And so have I. We don't know each other as well as we once did. We need to take our time. We need to…"

She let the sentence fade, feeling as though her bumbling discourse sounded much too lame for belief. Surely he'd see her plea for what it truly was…pure evasion.

The kiss he gingerly placed on one corner of her mouth was so gentle, so sweet, her heart constricted with heavy guilt.

His green eyes were clear and shining with generosity as he said, "I'm happy to give us all the time you think we need."

Chapter Ten

She had to tell him. She simply had to tell him.

How could she not? How could she keep this secret from Dylan and expect them to share any kind of long-term, loving relationship? It would be impossible. Totally inconceivable.

Tess paced from one end of Dylan's kitchen to the other. She'd met Erin at the bus, fixed her a snack and then shooed the child up to her room to study for tomorrow's spelling test.

During the three days that had passed since Erin's birthday, Tess had stiffened each and every time Dylan had reached for her. She wanted so badly to feel his hands on her. But the guilty secret she harbored hovered continuously on the edges of her brain.

When she was alone in her hotel room, she'd allowed herself to dream of being with Dylan. Of the happy family life she, Dylan and Erin could have together. A ready-made family. She'd even gone so far as to plan exactly how to go about leaving the family medical practice in Connecticut and opening her own office here in Pine Meadow. There was certainly no reason why she couldn't. Her doctorate made her eligible to practice medicine anywhere. Of course, she'd have to look into procuring a state license...

But a heavy dark feeling in the pit of her gut burst the bubble of every happy dream she conjured, the dark feelings caused by the knowledge that she was concealing from Dylan the entire truth. The fact that she was saving him from being hurt didn't ease her guilt one iota. The secret she kept was like a towering mountain between her and Dylan. Between her and true happiness.

She simply had to tell him.

After she did, after they climbed the jagged, and most probably hurtful, cliffs representing the whole truth regarding the past, then and only then would they be free to plan their future together.

And, oh, what a future it would be.

Dylan pushed open the kitchen door, and Tess stopped dead in her tracks. His expression was grim, his stance tight with stress. The aura he presented, the mood fairly vibrating from him, was tense, pent-up, disapproving.

Tess's first thought was that he'd argued with one of his mechanics, or a customer. However, that thought turned doubtful when she became cognizant of his glare—a glare focused directly on her.

"What is it?" she asked. "What's wrong?"

"You didn't come back to Pine Meadow because of Erin."

His tone was low, ominous, and trepidation clenched in Tess's stomach as though it were a huge fist.

She frowned. "Of course, I didn't," she said. "I

told you from the very beginning that I didn't know about Erin until I saw her for the first time in your shop.''

"That's your story and you're sticking to it, huh?"

Tess's brow knitted with tighter creases and she nodded. Then she asked, "Is there some reason why I shouldn't?"

"You could say that."

It was when he lifted his arm a few inches that she noticed for the first time the papers he held in his hand.

"You want to try to explain this?" He tossed the loose pages onto the tile-topped island standing between them.

Tess reached out, not picking them up, but only turning them around to face her. Her eyes widened. There in front of her was her father's bank account information. Only her father's name wasn't listed on the account—*hers* was.

Dylan's mother must have gone into the computer at the bank and changed the name of the account holder...without Tess's permission. There had to be some sort of law against such an action.

"Why didn't you tell me you'd spoken with my mother?" he asked, accusation weighing heavy in his query.

Still reeling under the idea that Helen Minster could have done such a thing, Tess automatically answered, "Because I didn't want you to be hurt. I didn't want Erin to be hurt."

Or my father's memory to be defiled, the silent words died on her tongue. Tess doubted Dylan would be the least interested in her last reason for withholding information from him.

"At least you're owning up to knowing about the

account,'' he said. ''When Mom came to see me, she'd told me to expect you to deny any wrongdoing.''

Ten years ago, the only wrongdoing Tess could have been accused of would have been that of giving herself, body and soul, to the boy she'd loved. But here and now, she felt horribly guilty for having connived with that untrustworthy woman. For that, Tess felt just plain awful, especially when that unholy alliance—one she'd agreed to for what she'd thought were such noble reasons—was being used against her.

''I heard you tell Erin you'd come back to town because of some 'business papers' you'd found,'' Dylan continued. ''I never would have imagined Minster Savings and Loan business was what you meant.'' He glared. ''You came back for the money. Period.''

The allegation he charged her with was like the final slam of a judge's gavel. Verdict rendered. No further evidence allowed. No further arguments accepted.

She tipped up her chin, refusing to let him see how his words hurt her.

''I did not come back *for* the money,'' she said quietly. ''I came back *about* the money.''

''Don't waste my time with semantics!''

His shout actually made her jump.

''There's no need to raise your voice,'' she said. ''Erin will hear you.''

They both grew quiet and still when they heard Erin's rushed footfalls on the bare wood.

''Dad?'' Erin didn't come into the room, evidently feeling the angry tension pulsing in the air. Hovering in the doorway, she asked, ''Is everything okay?''

''Go back to your room, Erin.'' Dylan didn't take his hard gaze off Tess as he addressed his daughter behind him. ''I need to talk to your mother. Alone.''

''But...'' The child's voice faded.

The frown of confusion Tess saw on Erin's brow just about broke her heart.

"Mom, what's going on?"

"Honey, your dad and I need to talk," Tess said gently. "Listen to your dad. Go back to your room. I'll come back and say good-night before I leave. I promise."

"But I heard Dad yell."

"Erin." There was a clear warning in Dylan's voice. "Go."

The child hung her head and turned on her heel. Tess's heart ached to reassure Erin. To tell her that everything would be okay. But she couldn't. Because she didn't know if everything *would* be okay.

Dylan glanced at the empty hallway, then called out, "Shut your door," and immediately, the click of Erin's bedroom door latch sounded.

When he turned his eyes on Tess, she likened them to chips of cold stone.

"What I can't fathom," he said, "is why all the romantic games?"

His tone clearly conveyed that he was gaining momentum, that he didn't want her to answer, that he wanted to get his thoughts out into the open.

"Why would you go to the trouble of toying with my emotions, playing me for a fool, teasing me with your wiles, if all you were interested in was getting your hands on that money?" He rubbed at the back of his neck with one hand. "And then during the drive home, it dawned on me. You were retaliating. You were looking for some kind of revenge because I'd hurt you all those years ago when you left Pine Meadow."

His shoulders squared and he tipped up his chin just

enough to give Tess the impression that he was looking down on her.

"Well," he said, "your trip to Pine Meadow has been a complete success. You've brought me to my knees *and* you've procured your monetary reward for all the hardship you suffered over the past ten years."

His sarcasm was like a smack in the face.

"What I suggest you do," he said, "is take your money and get the hell out of Pine Meadow. You're not wanted here."

"That's not true!"

Erin ran from the hallway where she'd obviously been hiding, *and* eavesdropping.

"I want you to be here," Erin said, her voice bordering on hysteria as she threw her arms around Tess's waist. "I don't want you to go anywhere. I don't care what Dad says. You can't go. You can't!"

Tess's throat constricted. Erin's overwhelming anxiety made tears well up in her eyes. And those tears were blurring her vision as she looked over at Dylan.

His jaw knotted with emotion, anger at her, concern for their daughter, apprehension for the situation they found themselves in, Tess couldn't tell. All she knew was that she felt very irritated with him for not rushing to comfort Erin.

"Honey," she crooned, bending over and hugging the child tight to her chest, "it's going to be okay." She felt Erin's body trembling and knew how troubled her daughter was over the prospect of losing her mother just when they'd found each other.

"You promise?" Erin whispered against Tess's shirt.

"Of course I do," Tess said, leading Erin out of the room. "Come on. Let me take you to your room. Your dad and I can't talk this out unless you give us a little privacy.''

Once they were in Erin's bedroom, Tess settled her daughter into the desk chair. Then Tess squatted down and gazed into Erin's young, frightened eyes.

"Honey, this problem is between me and your dad,'' Tess explained. "It has nothing to do with you.''

"But Dad's shouting.''

"Well,'' Tess said, "he's angry. And people sometimes shout when they're angry. But he's not angry with you. And neither am I. We both love you very much.'' She smoothed her fingertips over Erin's forearm. "Now I don't want you to worry. We'll work this out.''

"He told you to go away.''

Tess smiled, and she knew the monumental power of her maternal love for her child shone through her eyes. "Nothing and no one will ever be able to separate us, Erin. Do you believe me?''

Erin nodded silently.

"And didn't I already promise that I wouldn't leave town without saying goodbye?''

Again, Erin nodded.

"I want you to trust me.'' Tess stood up and planted a gentle kiss on top of her daughter's head. "I also want you to study hard so you can get an *A* on your spelling test. Just for me.''

Tess went to the door.

"Mom?''

She turned back. "Yes, sweetie?''

"I'll get an *A*,'' Erin whispered. "Just for you.''

After blowing her daughter a kiss, she closed Erin's door and made her way back toward the kitchen.

She pondered her next move. She could go back in

that room and plead her case; she could tell him her side of the story in the hopes of clearing her name. Or she could let him go on believing whatever awful things his mother had told him.

Of one thing she was completely sure—she was sick to death of being judged. And it was at that moment, when she stood in the kitchen doorway and Dylan's eyes bored into her, that she was struck with a sudden, life-altering realization. One she couldn't possibly keep to herself.

"All those years ago when you and I dated," she began, wanting him to understand the full impact of her revelation when she finally revealed it, "I was made to feel that I wasn't good enough. By your parents. And by you. Everyone was giving me the message that I was unworthy of you."

Dylan looked clearly taken aback. "I never felt you weren't good enough. Never."

"Oh, yes, you did." She crossed her arms tightly over her chest. "Otherwise, we wouldn't have had to keep our relationship a secret from your parents."

"We kept our relationship from your father, too," he said pointedly.

"But you know very well that we did that because you were three years older than I was. He would never have allowed his fifteen-year-old daughter to date an eighteen-year-old young man. Would you allow that situation to develop for Erin?" Before he had a chance to answer, she raised her brows and said, "If you're entirely truthful here, you'll admit that you didn't want to tell your parents about us because you *knew* they wouldn't approve of me."

He averted his guilty gaze to the floor for a split second and then directed his eyes back to her face.

"With your silence," she continued, "you relayed the clear message to me that you agreed with them."

Dylan's tone was low as he said, "You're wrong. I didn't agree with them. That wasn't the message I meant to convey."

"Ah, but to me, the important thing is," she said, "that's the message *I received.* And worse, that's the message *I believed.*" Almost to herself, she said, "All my life, I've felt...unworthy. Not good enough."

The ire she'd been holding at bay, burst forth, like water rushing over a dam.

"But walking down that hallway just now," she said, "I was overcome with the most marvelous thought. It doesn't matter what you think of me. It doesn't matter what your mother thinks of me. What matters is what *I* think of me." She leveled her gaze on him. "That's what should have mattered to me all along. If I'd made my own opinion more important than everyone else's, I'd have been so much better off."

Leaning against the kitchen counter, Dylan said, "So let me get this straight. Because my parents made you feel inferior, because you claim that I've made you feel inferior, then you think that makes it okay for you to lie, to cheat, to steal? You still haven't explained that," he said, pointing to the bank papers he'd brought home with him.

"Dylan, I have no intention of explaining anything to you."

"You don't have to," he said. "The evidence pretty much speaks for itself."

Tess walked to the table, picked up her purse and slid the long leather strap over one shoulder. "I'm so glad this came to light before anything really developed between us. I'd hate to have to go through life feeling the need to explain myself, feeling beholden and eternally grateful to the man who was supposed to love me for who I am.''

"Who you are?" He sounded incredulous. "I'm still trying to figure that out. You said the years that have passed have made a difference in us. I didn't want to believe it, but now I can finally agree. I don't know you."

Tess went to the back door and turned the knob, then turned to face him once again. "I'm sure you don't. But you *do* know your mother."

She glanced at the papers sitting untouched on the tiled counter, then she looked back at him. "Delve a little further," she advised, her tone as cool and smooth as polished granite. She wouldn't let Dylan, or any other Minster for that matter, ever hurt her again. "Dig a little deeper. You just might learn something important."

With that, she walked out, shutting the door firmly behind her.

The paperwork was complete. Tess signed the official document that would transfer her father's savings account in Minster Savings and Loan into Erin's name. Sliding the paper into the manila folder along with the small black bankbook, Tess was relieved to have the matter of the money settled once and for all. The account would serve as the beginnings of a college fund for her daughter. That solution made the most logical sense to Tess.

Dropping into Dylan's lap the responsibility for making the transfer was Tess's way of being absolutely sure he'd discover the real truth about the money—and about the past. She planned to slip the manila envelope containing the transfer document and the bankbook into his mailbox on her way out of town.

Tess picked up the white envelope, the goodbye note she'd written to Erin snug inside. The words had been slow in coming, agonizingly hard to write, as Tess had reflected on the deep, incomparable love she'd discovered over the past few weeks since learning she was a mother.

She hoped Erin would understand her motives behind leaving Pine Meadow so quickly, too quickly to say goodbye face-to-face. Once she was back in Connecticut, Tess would call her daughter every single day. She'd promised Erin so in the note.

Pressing the letter to her heart, Tess prayed that Dylan would see to it that Erin received her heartfelt message. Then she slipped the note in the manila envelope with the bank papers, sealed it and wrote Dylan's name on the front.

The suitcase latches clicked with a depressing finality as she snapped them closed.

Don't look at this like it's an ending, she told herself. Look at it as a new beginning.

She and Dylan were a thing of the past. It was silly of her to have thought otherwise. Her relationship with him had been over years ago. Neither one of them could change that.

But her relationship with Erin was only just beginning, and that was something to be joyous about.

Picking up her suitcase and the manila envelope, she gave the hotel room one last look, and then stepped out into the crisp fall air.

The leaves on the trees lining the highway were just beginning to turn crimson and burnt orange, and Tess rolled down her car window, hoping the cool autumn air might lift her spirits.

An hour later, she pulled off the road at a rest stop for a bite to eat. It wasn't that she was hungry, really, she simply couldn't bring herself to cross the boundary and leave the state of New Jersey. Maybe after a little fortification, she could tackle the obstacle the state line posed.

After lingering over a second cup of coffee, she decided she'd dawdled long enough. It was time to get back on the road.

Tess hadn't been driving twenty minutes before she noticed car lights flashing in her rearview mirror. For a moment, she thought the police may be signaling her to pull over. But then she saw it wasn't a traffic cruiser but a regular car. Well, not a regular car. It was a souped-up, canary-yellow roadster, hot on her tail.

Dylan had followed her.

Tess glared into the rearview mirror. He'd read the note she'd written to Erin. Tess just knew it. And he'd chased her down with the intention of changing her plans.

She pulled her car to the shoulder of the road. The roadster pulled over behind her.

From the side mirror on her door, she watched him exit his car and walk toward hers. Lord, he looked so good, she thought. Tall and dark and too damned handsome for words. But then a flaring anger took total control of her emotions. How dare he hunt her down like this?

She threw open her car door, storming to a stand. "Just what do you think you're doing? You read Erin's letter, didn't you? Well, you can't change my mind. I'm going to Connecticut to sell my father's house and resign from my practice and then I'm coming back to Pine Meadow. I'm going to open up an office in the Bowers. You—or your mother—can't keep me out of Pine Meadow. I'm going to see my daughter *every single day*. And nothing you can do or say will stop me.''

Just then the front passenger door of the roadster opened and Erin jumped out of the car. She ran around to greet her mother.

''Erin!''

Dylan and Tess grabbed for their daughter at the same time and pulled her to safety on the far side of the parked cars where the grass met the shoulder of the road.

''Honey, that was dangerous,'' Tess gently admonished, her heart pounding a furious beat.

''You can't run out in the road like that.'' Then Dylan asked Erin, ''Are you okay?''

''Sure,'' Erin answered with a small shrug. ''Gosh, adults are so uptight. I was being careful.''

After Tess heaved a sigh of relief, she realized that all the anger in her was gone, and she felt confused. Why would Dylan bring Erin if he meant to argue with her about her plans to return to Pine Meadow. She looked down at Erin and then up at Dylan. ''What are you two doing here?''

Erin quickly piped up, ''Dad's sorry he shouted at you last night. He didn't mean all those awful things he said. He told me he wanted to—''

''Hold it!'' Dylan interrupted the child. ''Erin, I really do appreciate your wanting to help here, but if you don't mind, this is something I need to do on my own.''

Tess didn't move. She didn't know what to think, what to say about the unexpected event unfolding before her. She saw her daughter's big brown eyes glitter with excitement.

Erin lifted her shoulders and let them drop. ''Sure, Dad,'' she said. ''Whatever you want.''

''Thanks.'' Dylan's voice was tinged with a mixture of chagrin and more than a little trepidation.

He waited a moment, and then looked down at Erin.

''Would you mind getting lost?'' he asked. ''Go get in the car. I'd like a little privacy.''

''*Da-ad*, we're parked on the side of the highway,'' she said. ''How much privacy do you think you're gonna get?'' After huffing an exasperated sigh, Erin went to the roadster and climbed inside.

Awkwardness hummed between Tess and Dylan, along with that ever-present attraction. She hated the fact that he still fascinated her so, even after all they'd been through, even after all the pain she'd suffered and even though she had no idea whatsoever of what was happening here.

''I did read the note you dropped off for Erin,'' he said.

There was something in his tone that made her pulse quicken with some mysterious emotion. Hope? Anticipation?

Don't be silly, she told herself.

''I came home to pick her up after school,'' he told her, ''and I found the envelope you left.''

He paused, and time ticked slowly by. Tess moistened her lips. Feeling the need to fill up the silence, she said, ''When I realized it was you following me, I assumed you were chasing me down to talk me out of coming back to Pine Meadow.''

''No.'' He shook his head. ''That's not why I came.''

''Erin said you came to apologize for shouting at me last night,'' she said. ''You didn't need to drive to the state line for that.'' Her tone lowered an octave.

"Especially when you knew I was coming back. What you had to say could have waited."

"No," he repeated, this time more emphatically, "it couldn't wait."

"Oh."

They looked at each other. Waiting.

"Tess," he finally said, "I've been such an idiot. I don't know if you can ever forgive me, but I hope you'll try."

Her heart hammered with excitement. But she refused to assume that his apology was anything more than that. A simple apology.

Offering him a small smile, she said, "You're forgiven. We need to get along, you and I. We have a daughter that needs raising."

His groan disclosed real agony. "Please don't tell me that Erin is the only reason you think we need to get along."

A giddiness jittered in her stomach. But still she felt the need to play it cool.

"Since you came back to town—" Dylan stepped closer to her, cupped her elbows in the palms of his hands "—I've had a small taste of what life might have been like for us if all that rotten stuff hadn't happened. If our parents hadn't pulled us apart."

He gazed into her eyes. "I know all about it. My mother was in tears when I finally forced the full truth out of her."

"Oh, Dylan, I'm sorry." The words were out of Tess's mouth before she could think. "I was going to tell you. I knew I was going to have to. Especially when we grew closer with each passing day. But I didn't want you to be hurt. And you would have been when you discovered what your mother, our parents, had done, and—'' she paused ''—I didn't want you to think badly of my father.''

Her explanation seemed jumbled, confused, but from the look on his face, she knew he understood.

''Unfortunately I do realize that everyone concerned, your dad, my parents, were doing what they thought was best for us.'' He sighed. ''There's simply no excuse for my mother's actions, ten years ago or a few days ago. But the fact that your father could never bring himself to spend the money has to say something in his favor, don't you think?''

Tess looked down at the ground. ''But I've missed so much. So much of Erin's life.''

''It breaks my heart to think about that,'' he said softly. ''I'm so sorry you were lied to. Hell, I'm sorry *I* was lied to.'' He squeezed her arms just enough to get her to look into his eyes. ''I'm sorry I didn't believe you when you said you'd been told that Erin hadn't survived her birth. But most of all...''

The intensity in his gaze had Tess mesmerized.

''I'm sorry that I didn't believe *in* you when my mother was maligning your character yet again just yesterday. You were so right. I do know her. I know what kind of person she is. I should have known better than to listen to her.''

After a moment, Tess couldn't help but remark ''The world just seems to be against us.''

''Oh, no,'' he said. ''Not the whole world. That little girl back there, she's for us. One hundred percent.''

A smile curled Tess's lips. ''She's a sweetheart.''

''She loves you,'' Dylan said. Then he added, ''I love you.''

Her breath caught in her throat. Had he really spoken those three little words?

Somehow she found herself in his arms, hugging him like there was no tomorrow.

"I couldn't let you go off without telling you," he whispered against her ear.

"Oh, Dylan," she said, tears of joy welling in her eyes, emotion lumping in her throat, "I love you. I've always loved you. I don't think I ever stopped."

He kissed her then, right there on the side of the highway, his mouth desperate and hungry.

"If you guys can quit being mushy for a minute," Erin called from the car window, "I have something I want to tell Mom."

"Can't it wait?" Dylan growled good-naturedly. "I'm busy here."

Tess chuckled. "What is it, honey?" she asked Erin.

"I got an *A* on my spelling test."

"Wow! That's great," Tess said.

"Life is great!" Dylan shouted for all the world to hear, and he picked up Tess and whirled her around in a circle.

Throwing her head back, Tess laughed with abandon. And she knew with no uncertainty that her small family would beat all the odds fate or the world could throw at them. All the wrongs of the past had been righted, all the secrets revealed. The happiness she had found with Dylan and Erin was more than enough to last a lifetime.

*   *   *   *   *

Silhouette ROMANCE™

SOMETIMES THE SMALLEST PACKAGES CAN LEAD TO THE BIGGEST SURPRISES!

Join *Silhouette Romance*
as more couples experience
the joy only babies
can bring!

Bundles of Joy

July 1999
BABIES, RATTLES AND
CRIBS... OH MY!
by Leanna Wilson (SR #1378)

His baby girl had suddenly appeared on his doorstep, and Luke Crandall needed daddy lessons—fast! So lovely Sydney Reede agreed to help the befuddled bachelor. But when baby cuddles turned into grown-up kisses, Sydney wondered if what Luke really wanted was *her!*

August 1999
THE BILLIONAIRE AND THE BASSINET
by Suzanne McMinn (SR #1384)

When billionaire Garrett Blakemore set out to find the truth about a possible heir to his family's fortune, he didn't expect to meet a pretty single mom and her adorable baby! But the more time he spent with Lanie Blakemore and her bundle of joy, the more he found himself wanting the role of dad....

And look for more **Bundles of Joy** titles in late 1999:

THE BABY BOND by Lilian Darcy (SR #1390)
in September 1999

BABY, YOU'RE MINE by Lindsay Longford (SR #1396)
in October 1999

Available at your favorite retail outlet.

Silhouette®

Looking For More Romance?

Visit Romance.net

Check in daily for these and other exciting features:

Hot off the press

View all current titles, and purchase them on-line.

What do the stars have in store for you?

Horoscope

Hot deals

Exclusive offers available only at Romance.net

Plus, don't miss our interactive quizzes, contests and bonus gifts.

PWEB

Available July 1999 from Silhouette Books...

World's Most
Eligible Bachelors

AGENT OF
THE BLACK WATCH
by BJ JAMES

Black Watch

The World's Most Eligible Bachelor:

Secret-agent lover Kieran O'Hara was on a desperate mission.
His objective: Anything but marriage!

Kieran's mission pitted him against a crafty killer...and
the prime suspect's beautiful sister. For the first time in his
career, Kieran's instincts as a man overwhelmed his lawman's
control...and he claimed Beau Anna Cahill as his lover. But
would this innocent remain in his bed once she learned his
secret agenda?

**Each month, Silhouette Books brings you an
irresistible bachelor in these all-new, original
stories. Find out how the sexiest, most-sought-after men
are finally caught....**

Available at your favorite retail outlet.

Everybody's favorite family is back—the Reeds.

HOLDING OUT FOR A HERO

Coming in June 1999

Three complete, unforgettable novels by bestselling storyteller

GINA WILKINS

You'll love these stories about how the three Reed sisters, Summer, Spring and Autumn hold out for heroes!

Available at your favorite retail outlet.

HARLEQUIN®
Makes any time special ™

Coming in June 1999 from

Silhouette Books...

Those matchmaking folks at Gulliver's Travels are at it again—and look who they're working their magic on this time, in

HOLIDAY *Honeymoons*

Two Tickets to Paradise

For the first time anywhere, enjoy these two new complete stories in one sizzling volume!

HIS FIRST FATHER'S DAY   Merline Lovelace
A little girl's search for her father leads her to
Tony Peretti's front door...and leads *Tony* into the
arms of his long-lost love—the child's mother!

MARRIED ON THE FOURTH   Carole Buck
Can summer love turn into the real thing? When
it comes to Maddy Malone and Evan Blake's
Independence Day romance, the answer is a
definite "yes!"

Don't miss this brand-new release—
HOLIDAY HONEYMOONS: Two Tickets to Paradise—
coming June 1999, only from Silhouette Books.

Available at your favorite retail outlet.

*This June 1999, the legend
continues in Jacobsville*

Diana Palmer

LONG, TALL TEXANS
EMMETT, REGAN & BURKE

This June 1999, Silhouette brings readers
an extra-special trade-size collection
for Diana Palmer's legion of fans.
These three favorite Long, Tall Texans
stories have been brought back in
one collectible trade-size edition.

*Emmett, Regan & Burke are about to be led
down the bridal path by three irresistible women.
Get ready for the fireworks!*

**Don't miss this collection of favorite
Long, Tall Texans stories…
available in June 1999
at your favorite retail outlet.**

**Then in August 1999 watch for
LOVE WITH A LONG, TALL TEXAN
a trio of brand-new short stories featuring
three irresistible Long, Tall Texans.**